"THERESE, LET'S HAVE DINNER MONDAY NIGHT," HE said.

She rummaged idly with the gadgets in her desk drawer and came out with a paper clip, which she began to bend. The arrival of the painting's owner somehow changed the intimacy that had developed between them. "We've already had takeout," she said. "Remember? That was your way of clearing the air between us."

"This will be at a real restaurant. Just us. Regular air. I promise."

She pursed her lips, considering. "Give me one good reason why I should go with you."

"You like to eat."

She smiled slowly. "This is true."

"You can have all the cheesecake with chocolate-cookie crust that you can eat," he promised.

She was strangely touched that he remembered. "Good memory."

"You don't have to pay for your half of the check," he added.

"Now, that's a compelling reason," she said, and he chuckled.

"I'll get you from the museum at six," he told her.

"What is this masterful tone?" she objected. "Is that supposed to be cool or something? Do you practice it? Is it like your macho driving?"

He groaned. "Would you just say yes for once?"

"No," she said, smiling.

But she was pretty sure he got the idea. . .

WHAT ARE *LOVESWEPT* ROMANCES?

They are stories of true romance and touching emotion. We believe those two very important ingredients are constants in our highly sensual and very believable stories in the LOVE-SWEPT line. Our goal is to give you, the reader, stories of consistently high quality that may sometimes make you laugh, sometimes make you cry, but are always fresh and creative and contain many delightful surprises within their pages.

Most romance fans read an enormous number of books. Those they truly love, they keep. Others may be traded with friends and soon forgotten. We hope that each LOVESWEPT romance will be a treasure—a "keeper." We will always try to publish

LOVE STORIES YOU'LL NEVER FORGET
BY AUTHORS YOU'LL ALWAYS REMEMBER

The Editors

Loveswept® 881

MASTER TOUCH

CARAGH M. O'BRIEN

BANTAM BOOKS
NEW YORK · TORONTO · LONDON · SYDNEY · AUCKLAND

MASTER TOUCH

A Bantam Book / March 1998

ISBN 0-553-44634-7

Published simultaneously in the United States and Canada

---

*Bantam Books are published by Bantam Books, a division of Bantam Dou-
bleday Dell Publishing Group, Inc. Its trademark, consisting of the words
"Bantam Books" and the portrayal of a rooster, is Registered in U.S. Patent
and Trademark Office and in other countries. Marca Registrada. Bantam
Books, 1540 Broadway, New York, New York 10036.*

PRINTED IN THE UNITED STATES OF AMERICA

OPM   0 9 8 7 6 5 4 3 2 1

For Joe

PROLOGUE

As Therese Carroll stepped into the office, A. K. Lewison walked around his desk and extended both hands toward her. His thick glasses magnified his eyes and made the rest of his elderly face look small; his welcome was genuine and warm.

"Good to see you," he said. "Are those earrings or fishing lures you've got there?"

Therese laughed, shaking her head so that the light reflected off her silver earrings and the cool metal whispered against her neck. The earrings matched a fish pattern on her blue silk jacket, one of her favorites.

"My aunt sent them from São Paulo," she said. "You want to borrow them when you go fishing?"

He shook his head. "I'd look a little silly."

"Only if you wore them," Therese said, smiling.

Whenever Therese saw her late father's friend, her pleasure was tinged by a trace of loss, as if her father should be with them in the sunny, book-lined office. Even when the two old college friends had lived hundreds of miles apart, they had shared an ongoing exchange of aged wine, legal advice, and adventure stories. She smiled at A.K., guessing that he missed her father too, and moved to where the February sunlight warmed a row of hardy spider plants.

"So are you curious enough yet?" A.K. asked. "Did you ever expect to get such a fax?"

In abbreviated, cryptic sentences, as if the sender were more accustomed to sending telegrams, a fax had asked her to meet "Parisian art dealer M. Dansforth, former friend of Harry Carroll. Noon, February 13, Lewison's." Therese had been intrigued and somewhat amused.

"Did he really know my father?" she asked.

"Seems to have. He has a restoration project for you," A.K. said. "An interesting one, I believe."

Soon after Therese had begun her fellowship at the renowned Bay State Art Museum five years earlier, shortly after her father's death, she had been hailed as one of the most talented, painstaking art conservators the museum had seen in years. While most of her friends from graduate school were still bouncing from fellowship to fellowship, she had been hired permanently, and she was keenly aware of how fortunate she was. Quietly driven, sincerely devoted to restoring old paintings, Therese often worked long hours and weekends. It didn't leave her much time for moonlighting.

Or even plain moonlight, she thought wryly. She couldn't remember the last time she'd gazed at a star or relaxed with a good book.

"So where is he?" she asked. She reflexively reached for her braid and smoothed it forward, sliding her hand down the rope of dark hair.

A.K. opened his hands. "Maybe he's looking for a parking space?"

She grimaced. "That should only take him an eternity."

"Half an hour, actually," said a man from the doorway.

She turned at hearing the low, resonant voice and lifted her chin in an unconscious gesture of assessment.

Milo Dansforth closed the heavy door behind him, and in three long, leisurely strides he was before her, holding out a hand. With a faint jingle of her bracelets, she put out her own hand and felt it clasped in a warm, strong grasp. Secretly she was surprised. She'd assumed Milo would be older, closer to A.K.'s age, but this man wasn't even thirty-five, she guessed, quickly taking in an impression of thick brown hair and steady eyes.

He released her hand, and as he removed his coat and walked back to the curved wooden coat rack by the door, she had a chance to study him.

Clean-cut profile, nonstraight nose, she thought. He was definitely tall enough. His broad, square shoulders hunched slightly with casual grace as he slid one arm and then the other out of his coat. His brown hair was parted on the side and lay easily back from his hairline to show a slight thinning above his temples. Nothing boyish there, she mused. As he turned and came forward again, his trousers ran true down to his black wingtips, every line of him meticulously neat. She looked back up at those shoulders covered in impeccable wool and decided his look wasn't merely conservative, but classic. An unexpected tug of attraction caught her off guard, and she rolled her lips inward. He was going to smile, she thought.

But he didn't. Milo was studying her so intently that it was almost rude. It was her coloring, she figured, guessing he had not expected her Brazilian-American heritage. Her father had come from an old Irish, Minnesota background, but Therese strongly favored her Brazilian relatives on her mother's side. If Milo was looking for a resemblance to his old friend, he was going to be disappointed. Therese straightened with unconscious pride, subtly daring him to recognize the femininity of her graceful form, and she saw his gaze sharpen, his eyes flicking to hers.

Her body tightened with a minute, electric response, and for a flashing instant she had the feeling she knew him. But that was impossible.

"It's a pleasure to finally meet you," he said.

"Especially after spending half an hour cruising for a free parking meter," she said, smiling.

Milo looked surprised. "The meter turned into a parking lot," he explained.

She laughed. "Lucky you. My meter just has delusions of grandeur. And it's doomed to expire no matter what it thinks."

A.K. chuckled from across the room, but Milo only gave her a quizzical look.

Obviously no sense of humor, she thought.

With a brief knock on the door, A.K.'s secretary looked in. "I'm sorry to interrupt," she said to A.K. "Would you have a minute? Your one o'clock appointment is here early."

A.K. looked startled, then nodded. "If you'll excuse

me," he said to Therese and Milo. "I'll only be a minute." He adjusted his glasses and hurried out the door.

With A.K.'s departure, Therese felt a subtle increase in the tension in the room and she instinctively crossed her arms. Milo paced closer to the windows, so that one of his shoes fell in a rectangle of sunlight on the carpet.

"Since your meter's ticking, let me explain a couple things and get to the point," he began. "I knew your father in Romania fifteen years ago, when he was smuggling art out of the country."

Therese felt her eyebrows lift. It wasn't exactly common knowledge that her father, a respected art dealer, had also spent two years as a smuggler. Her father had long believed important European artworks were in jeopardy, and when she was still a child, he had worked hard to recover certain paintings for their original owners. That much she knew, and whatever boundaries he had had to cross, she was convinced her father had never done anything unethical.

"I believe my father was visiting Romania as a scholar at that time," she said.

"He was smuggling paintings, and he needed a guide."

Therese laughed. "You're telling me you were my father's guide when he smuggled paintings out of Romania? Excuse me if I'm skeptical. For one, you're American, aren't you? And fifteen years ago you couldn't have been out of high school."

Milo took another pace into the sunshine, so Therese saw an angle of light cut midway up his trousers. "I was seventeen to be exact," he said. "And I had lived in

Romania for several years. I knew my way around. Your father believed I could help him, and I did, in a way."

Therese turned slightly from the bookshelf so that she could face him as he stepped farther into the sunlight. "Let's hear it," she said. "Especially the 'in a way' part."

"I should begin at the end, I suppose." He frowned at one of the spider plants, then peered over at her. "Fifteen years ago, a lifetime ago, I worked with your father in Bucharest. It was around the time of the winter solstice, and it was cold. The city was constantly having electricity failures, and it seemed I always met your father in the dark. It's his voice I remember best."

Milo frowned again at the spider plant, while Therese heard a lost echo of her father's voice. She felt the hairs lift on the back of her neck. "Go on," she said.

"One night your father and I were in the basement of a deserted mansion. We'd stored half a dozen paintings there, ready for exportation. At least two of the paintings are now priceless, but then they were simply unknown artworks; incredibly beautiful, riveting paintings." His voice softened. He turned his face toward her again, and she felt the full intensity of his gaze. "Your father would have died for those paintings."

Therese looked down, touched by his impression of her father. She knew it was no exaggeration. Some paintings her father would have died for, they had moved him so. Art was like a drug to him, or more: an elemental sustenance. And Milo Dansforth, this unlaughing, stone-like individual, had known and understood her father's passion. She found the contradiction unnerving, and she never liked being unnerved.

"Apparently he didn't die for those particular paintings," she said. "What happened?"

"The authorities cornered us in the basement. We knew they would search until they found someone, but they didn't need to catch us both. Who was I? Just a kid in trouble. But Harry had a family." Milo dropped one hand into his pants pocket. "He had you."

Therese resisted a feeling of loss. She missed her father, more than she cared to think, and Milo's words were reopening a wound that had never fully healed. Her instinct was to cover her pain with a joke, so she laughed.

"I was a real prize back then," she said dryly. "Braces and nerdy glasses and a rebellious streak that nearly put my grandparents in their graves."

"He talked about you all the time."

"Every father talks about his kids."

"He kept saying that he was going to miss seeing you in a play."

That stopped her cold. Her father had missed her appearance as the Scarecrow in her school production of *The Wizard of Oz*, even though he'd promised to be there. The event had been keenly memorable to her, and yet shortly afterward her disappointment had been overshadowed by an increasing fear that he might never return. Weeks had passed without word. A month. She'd hounded her grandparents with questions they couldn't answer. And then, finally, her father had come home, worn down but alive.

Therese straightened, alert to her own memories. There was some story she couldn't quite recall. Something about a boy named Peter or Pedro. Could Milo's story really be true?

"He did miss my play," she said quietly. "What happened that night in the basement?"

Milo came a step nearer, and with the sunlight hitting his face from the side, his eyes seemed strangely lit with energy.

"I told your father to hide in the wine cellar. He refused. He was paralyzed between wanting to save the paintings and wanting to escape to get back to you, and he couldn't do both. I could see the flashlights of the police coming, so I hit your father on the head and stuffed him back in the wine cellar behind some cartons. I hid one of the paintings with him, too, just before the police came."

Therese shook her head, unwilling to believe such a crazy story. Her father had been sick when he came home from Romania, and he wouldn't talk about what had happened there except to say that it was his great failure. She remembered her grandparents had been worried about him, and he'd had bad spells of insomnia. But still, none of this proved he'd been mixed up with Milo.

She frowned down at A.K.'s desk and picked up a stone paperweight. "I'm sorry," she said. "A.K. should have told you. I'm extremely overextended at the museum right now, and even if you knew my father, I'm not—"

He cut her off. "I have located the painting I hid with your father that last night in Romania."

She flashed her gaze to his face. "Where?" she asked. "How?"

"That doesn't matter. What matters is that I have it, and no one is going to take it again."

His obsessive tone made Therese want to laugh.

"Thanks for the warning," she said. "Should I assume you want me to restore it?"

"I don't 'want' you to restore it," he said with deceptive calm. "You *must* restore it."

She did laugh this time, with genuine pleasure. Of all the authoritarian, humorless men, he had to take the cake.

"Must," she echoed. "Such a popular word among tyrants. Or is it skydivers? 'Must' always means someone's neck is at stake."

He seemed to restrain himself with an effort. "You can spare me the sarcasm; I take your point. Please. Is that better?"

" 'Please' is always nice," she said, then felt her neck warm as she realized the residual humor in her voice had made the words come out in a low, inviting tone.

His narrowed eyes glowed strangely, then he turned to look out the window. Therese swallowed hard and tried to put her finger on the enigmatic tension she felt between them. There was more to his story than he was telling her. She was certain of that, but that wasn't what bothered her. Milo himself was the culprit, with the odd, magnetic quality he had, even when he didn't smile. Something about him made her want to tease him, she realized. Or strangle him. Either impulse was dangerous.

When he turned to face her again, his penetrating gray eyes were fierce in their determination.

"My pocket is deep enough to make a significant contribution to the museum on your behalf," he said. "It's deep enough to pay for your replacement at the museum or to pay off your boss directly. You can name your own salary. Anything."

His change in tactics caught her completely off guard, and she searched his face, hoping to find he wasn't serious. What she saw there chilled her.

"I see we're finally getting to the point," she said. She trailed a finger along A.K.'s desk and schooled her expression into neutral lines. "And this painting is in France?"

"Yes. My home is in Paris," he said. "I would expect you to travel with me there."

"Of course." Abandon everything she had there in Boston, she thought. "And when would this restoration begin?"

Milo looked grimly satisfied. "This afternoon. Monday at the latest."

Therese struggled to maintain her neutral expression and sustain the charade, but inside her ache of disappointment made her feel slightly ill.

All the magnetism he'd had when he'd talked about her father in Romania vanished when he talked about money. He sincerely believed that money alone could persuade her. She looked up at him once more, searching his cold, unyielding eyes, then she turned away.

"I'm sorry," she said. "It's impossible. You'll have to buy someone else."

In one long stride he was beside her, catching her slender arm so that she could feel his grip through the sleeve of her silk jacket.

"You're making a mistake," he said, a dangerous edge to his voice. "I need your help with this. I need it now."

Her anger fused into dignity as she refused to give him the satisfaction of trying to pull free, but inwardly she seethed. Although he was exerting a minimum of pressure on her arm, blistering lines of sensitivity were fanning out from his touch.

"Release me." She could feel her eyes burning with rage.

After one long, charged moment, he let go of her and shoved both hands in his pockets.

Therese backed away. Her cheeks burned with the heat of her anger, and she rubbed her arm where he had touched her, still feeling the impression. Milo's face was an impenetrable mask.

Just then, A.K. came back in, mumbling an apology. She saw annoyance flash across Milo's face, but she felt only relief.

"So are you going to restore Milo's painting?" A.K. asked. "Doesn't it sound fascinating?"

"No," she said.

She moved to pick up her purse while A.K. looked quickly from her to Milo.

"What's happened?" he asked.

"Mr. Bulldozer here needs a couple of lessons in persuasion, that's all," Therese said.

"Wait," Milo said.

She turned to face him, rigidly controlling her anger. "I have nothing more to say to you. And you have forfeited any right to my attention."

Milo took a step nearer, all formality gone, a certain desperation in his eyes. She could see his chagrin in the ruddiness of his complexion, but she didn't trust him at all.

"No, please, think again," he urged her. "I'm sorry. I didn't mean to— It's just hard for me to believe Harry Carroll's only daughter would be so unwilling to help me.

He would have died if he'd been caught and taken to prison!"

"Really," she said, stung. "My father was a survivor. He probably would have been better off in jail than he was getting knocked out by you. That is, if I can even believe you hid him in a wine cellar."

"I did! And he wouldn't have survived prison there. Not for three years."

She laughed scoffingly. "They don't lock up foreign scholars for three years. The embassy would have gotten him out."

"Then why didn't they get me out?"

She took a long look at him. "You're telling me you spent three years in a Romanian jail for my father? And he never even bothered to mention your name to me? That only proves you didn't know him. He would never be so ungrateful."

Milo stepped toward her again, and she flinched back a pace. He looked as if he would devour her if he could.

"Pablo," he said. "Your father called me Pablo."

Her mind triggered at the word: not on Pablo Picasso, but on the Pablo her father had called his savior, way back in the dimness of her childhood memory. Layers slipped back, like curtains pulling away from a tiny window.

"I'm only here thanks to Pablo," her weary father had said.

He'd whispered it to her that very first night he was home. She'd been asleep in her bed at her grandparents' house, but she'd felt her father enter the dim room, stepping through the back-lit doorway. He'd sat on the edge of her bed and taken her in his arms for his first homecoming hug. "Remember it, darling. Thanks to Pablo."

Slowly Therese walked back toward Milo, trying to see him clearly for who he was. If only she could erase the years from the mature man's face, if only she could see beneath the expensive suit and the polished, hardened exterior, she might find the passionate boy who had saved her father.

"Pablo," she mumbled to herself. "Thanks to Pablo."

His face opened with new hope as he watched her. The recklessness of the way he'd grabbed her earlier fit with the impetuousness of a boy who would have sacrificed himself for her father. And the name, Pablo, was a password of proof. It all fit. She had to believe him.

She slid into a chair, finally capitulating. "For my father's sake," she said, "I'll help you."

A.K. came forward, setting a hand on her shoulder. "I'm glad," he said. "I knew this had to be the man. Your father spoke to me about him, even if he never told you much. That's why I let him come here."

She looked up at Milo, whose rugged face was charged with contained energy. There was relief too, and unspoken gratitude. In fact, she thought, he looked dangerously human.

"This is wonderful," he said. "We can leave for Paris as soon as you're ready. I have a work studio all ready for you, and a flat with maid service and a chef—"

"Wait a second," she interrupted. "I'll help you, but I didn't say I was going to Paris. I can't just abandon my obligations at the museum. You bring the painting here to Boston, to the museum, and I'll do what I can. That's all I can promise."

Milo ran a hand through his dark hair, then braced his

fists on his hips. "The painting cannot be at the museum," he said.

"Why not? The conservation lab has all the supplies I need, and it would be perfectly safe."

"It's far too public a place."

"It's guarded twenty-four hours a day. I can promise you that if all the Sargents and Matisses are safe in the museum, your unknown Romanian picture will be safe there too."

He shook his head, and she could see the stubborn set of his chin. "No. I'm sorry. If you won't come to Paris, I'll rent a studio here in Boston, but the painting can't be in the museum lab, where anyone could find it."

She glanced expressively toward the ceiling. "I should have known we'd still be arguing. It's not enough for me to agree to do the work."

He was watching her, his expression quizzical. "We won't always be arguing," he said.

From him it was so mild, so unexpected, she laughed. "I'm glad you think so. Especially since it's so awful to argue long distance."

He seemed to hesitate, then spoke concisely. "There are other people interested in this painting. They might try to steal it. If they even just see it under the right conditions it could be costly. That's why I must insist on privacy. I'll come to Boston with the painting to oversee the work."

So much for keeping him an ocean away.

Milo began to tell her about the painting, a portrait from the early 1800s. A child bride named Louisa de Plentagon, who had married at thirteen and gone on to have fifteen children, had posed for the portrait just before her wedding.

"And the artist?" Therese asked.

"French. Soupçon, or possibly his student, Malgré." Milo's voice ran easily around the foreign syllables. "Soupçon was a master, and much of his apprentices' work is attributed to him, even when he added only the final touches."

It sounded fairly typical of the time, she thought. "The master touches," she said absently. "What makes this picture so special?"

He glanced toward the window, and his expression gradually eased. She saw a kind of expectation, a charmed pleasure transform his face, as if he were a child receiving a clever, unexpected gift. It still wasn't a smile, she thought, but in a way it was intriguing. When he looked back at her, he shook his head and shrugged one shoulder.

"I don't know how to describe it," he said, "but there's something unique about the painting. You'll see."

"I get the idea," she said. "My father had that same shrug. You're an art addict."

He didn't deny it. "There are worse things to be addicted to."

She laughed. "I know. I can see why my father liked you."

A brief frown touched his features but was gone before she could examine it. He looked down solemnly, then reached for her hand.

She almost pulled away, remembering the last time he'd touched her. He merely took her fingers into his own. She stood instinctively, rising from her chair to stand before him, but he lifted her fingers even higher and set a kiss on the back of her hand. A shiver of pleasure rode along her arm and she felt her cheeks warming at the unexpected intimacy of his gaze. He lowered her hand and smiled slightly, enigmatically.

She swallowed, feeling heat expanding inside her as he kept his hold on her fingers. Lifting her eyebrows, tilting her chin up, she waited for him to explain himself: his quaint, courtly gesture, his intense, possessive gaze. Gray, she thought, memorizing the color. His eyes were gray, like the color of ashes that hide hot coals.

"Perhaps there's a chance that you may like me too," he said, finally releasing her fingers. "Someday."

Oh, he was smooth, she thought. Way too smooth. If she didn't have a natural aversion to authority types, she'd be in deep trouble.

ONE

On a cold Saturday morning two weeks after that extraordinary meeting in A.K.'s office, Therese was preparing herself to meet Milo Dansforth again. Two days earlier he had left a key for her at the museum with a note saying the painting had arrived, he had rented a studio apartment on Commonwealth Avenue in Brookline, and would she care to meet him on Saturday. As she climbed the two flights of stairs to the apartment, her patterned mitten sliding easily up the smooth banister, she wondered if her father had ever dreamed she'd be returning a favor to Pablo. Her heart lightened at the prospect of an interesting new project, one that was linked with her father, however remotely. She wished she could remember more of his old story but couldn't. All that remained was a certainty that Pablo, now Milo Dansforth, had won her father's heartfelt respect and gratitude.

She took off her mitten and fingered the note. It gave no time, but it was now ten o'clock, a respectable hour. If he'd only given a phone number, too, she'd have called, but there was none. Sighing, she located a solid oak door, liking the brass knocker on it. Milo had picked a nice building, she thought, recently renovated by the looks of it. She fit the key in the lock and was turning the knob before it occurred to her that she ought to knock. With her belated knock, the unlatched door started to open, and a rustling noise from inside made her freeze.

"Hello?" she called.

"Is that Therese?"

She mentally groaned. Milo sounded sleepy.

"Should I come back later?" she asked.

"No. Just a minute. What time is it?"

"Ten," she said, certain now that she had woken him. "I'll come back later."

"No," he said again, and poked his head around the door.

Hair askew, the stubble of a night's sleep on his cheeks, Milo didn't look anything like the aloof, formal man she remembered. She couldn't keep herself from staring. He was, well, incredible. Beyond handsome. Heart-throb gorgeous. And really close. His wide-set gray eyes, fringed by long black eyelashes, were sleep-warmed and receptive. She hadn't expected this at all.

And then he smiled, a slow, almost shy curving of the lips, revealing even white teeth.

Therese had to lock her knees to keep from losing her balance.

"You look dazed," he said. "Did you just wake up?"

"Yes. I mean no," she muttered. How on earth had she failed to notice how incredibly handsome he was? His eyes were watchful, his smile an inviting line of mirth.

"Good," he said. "Because I just did and one of us is bad enough. Come on in."

He was holding the door open now and she slipped in past him, noting his chest was bare and a pair of black sweatpants was slung low on his trim hips. Blushing, she looked away, but not before she'd had a formidable first impression of his torso: lean, well muscled, and still touched by a fading tan. Glancing around the studio apartment, she found a double bed with a teak headboard standing in evocative disarray in one corner. By the windows, she noticed. And no curtains there.

"You like it?" he asked.

The bed? No, his torso. No, the room. "Of course," she said, quickly absorbing that half of the room was set up as a workspace.

"You'll have to excuse the attire. I overslept." He reached for a white T-shirt and pulled it over his head, so at least she could face him again without ogling his chest. Not that the close-fitting cotton did much to hide his physique.

"We'll need some blinds," she said, improvising. "The light is wonderful, but sunlight is actually bad for the paint."

"Blinds," he said. "Definitely."

She wondered if he was also thinking of the bed, and her gaze was drawn irresistibly to it. It was too easy to picture how he'd been there only minutes before, sleeping heavily in the tangle of a large down comforter. A quick glance at him showed her he was smiling again and watching her curiously.

"Second thoughts?" he asked.

"I didn't know you'd be living here," she managed to say.

"I'm not. Just for the next couple of days. I'm having a security guard come at nights, but he can't start until Monday and well . . ." He shrugged. "Jet lag," he apologized. "I was just so tired."

He rubbed fingers through his thick brown hair, then his lips curved in another smile. "Therese . . ." he began.

Startled by the personal tone in his voice, she waited, wary. He put his hands on his hips, then shook his head briefly.

"What is it?" she asked.

"I just never apologized sufficiently for grabbing your arm that day in A.K.'s office. It's bothered me ever since. I swore the first time I saw you again I'd tell you how sorry I am. I don't want you to think—"

She cut him off with a wave of her hand. "No need," she said.

He looked like he wanted to add more to his apology, but she was acutely uncomfortable with the topic. More than once in the last two weeks she'd replayed that moment in her mind, wondering at the residual tingling that remained in her nerves where his hand had encircled her arm. He hadn't held her hard, merely detained her really, yet something about his touch had stayed with her. It was the same with her hand, where he'd brushed a kiss on her knuckles.

"I just don't want you to think I'm a physical person," he said.

She took another long look at him—his raw strength and naturally athletic build, his poised chin and broad shoulders, the faintly visible pulse in the dip at the base of his neck—and laughed.

"You're not physical? Not at all?" she asked.

Color slowly washed into his unshaven cheeks, and he inhaled a long, full breath. "Right," he said. "Maybe I'll just shower. Look around. But don't open the crate. I want to show you Louisa myself."

He vanished behind a door, and she began to breathe normally again when she heard the prosaic noise of the toilet flushing.

This wasn't going to work, she thought. If she started indulging her libido with this man, even if the indulgence was only in her dreams, she was dead. And taunting him about not being physical when his body fairly screamed of virility and strength. What was that about? She groaned with delayed embarrassment. The man looked like a cross between Peter Weller and James Dean, with riveting eyes and dark, lazy sensuality. At least don't drool, Therese, she chastised herself.

But nothing had prepared her for the onslaught to her senses at finding him rumpled and rosy from sleep. She closed her eyes, shaking her head. What was she going to do?

He *had* to be less attractive when he came out of the shower, she told herself. That was all there was to it. She walked nervously around the room, waiting for the noise of the shower to stop while she took her bearings.

Half of the room had been set up as a workspace, not unlike what she was accustomed to at the museum lab. There were more sunlight and space, with light oak floors, a separate desktop area with a computer, and a kitchenette. The area around the bed had been furnished simply but with an eye for rich colors and textures. An Oriental carpet with turquoise and indigo threads linked the bed with a pair of straight-backed wooden chairs and a small table. A wooden chess set and a carefully folded newspaper lay on the table, as if someone had been playing out the daily game from the chess column.

She took off her coat and laid it across the back of one of the chairs. After a moment's hesitation, she unpacked a smock from the bag she'd brought and set that on the chair too.

She smoothed her fingers along the back of her hips, then hunched her shoulders to shake off her tension. Her braid of black hair swung forward, and she tightened the blue string that tied it. With her blue boots, the blue string, her black stretch pants, and gray cashmere pullover, she'd arranged a simple pattern of colors that pleased her and also emphasized the royal blue of her eyes.

Though it seemed to take forever, she knew his shower wasn't really lasting very long. Her boots made a hard, echoing sound on the wood floor as she crossed to the work area. She peered to read the labels on the bottles on the supply counter: ethanol, isopropyl alcohol. Beside them was a box of the giant cotton swabs she used for surface cleaning and a selection of fine-tipped brushes and paints. The other materials were there, too, everything she'd requested on the list she'd sent him, even the ultraviolet light. He'd spared no expense.

A large crate, its nails pried out, lay on an enormous table. She bent to peek in, but the edges revealed nothing to her. It smelled faintly of straw and pine.

She inhaled deeply, then paused, listening.

The shower had stopped, leaving a silence of anticipation that was even worse. When the bathroom door finally opened, she had an instant of fear that he might be in a towel, but he came through fully dressed, buttoning the sleeves of his white cotton shirt. His dark hair was combed back, still gleaming with wetness.

"Sorry to keep you waiting," he said.

Bad news, she thought. He was just as attractive fully clothed.

"No trouble," she said.

Box crease marks in his shirt showed that he didn't do his own laundry, but the jeans looked convincingly worn, comfortable. And trim in the seat, she noticed, when he turned to lean down for his shoes. There was no clue, no fancy watch, to give away that he must have resources in the millions.

He straightened, then walked closer. A waft of damp cleanliness came with him, the scent of shampoo and mint, and she could see he'd shaven.

"When did you get in from Paris?" she asked.

"Two days ago," he said, "when I left you the key. I meant to call about a time to meet today, but there was a problem with the jack and the line just came on late last night."

"That's okay." She wanted to ask him why he seemed so different, what had changed in the last two weeks so that he could smile now.

"What is it?" he asked.

She shook her head. "You just seem more relaxed than you did at A.K.'s office."

"You seem more uneasy."

She laughed. "Touché."

He ran a hand along his jaw, as if absently testing the closeness of his shave, while his eyes studied her curiously. "You laugh when you're uneasy," he remarked.

"If this is supposed to be putting me at my ease, it isn't working."

He nodded and dropped his gaze. "So do you want to see her?" he asked, walking over to the crate.

Relieved, she followed. The painting—the "she" to Milo—was bound to be neutral territory that would get Therese's mind back on work.

He moved around the table and touched the lid of the crate gingerly to be certain he had his hands in the right places. She stood opposite him, and together they lifted off the lid, revealing a layer of bubbled plastic. They set the lid aside and lifted the painting free to set it on the table. A fine layer of rice paper was all that covered the painting, and Therese stood beside him as he removed the delicate paper, pulling it aside to expose the painting of Louisa de Plentagon.

Therese squinted in approval while she critically took in the most conspicuous areas of damage. The painting was darkened overall, showing the telltale evidence of smoke damage. There was a slight "flap," a looseness of the canvas in the top left corner caused when the painting had been restretched on a new frame for some reason. She'd probably have to key that out. There were several faint streaks down the right-hand side, and it was likely the layer of soot concealed additional damage. She'd get a better idea after she'd inspected it with a black light, but for now, altogether, she was optimistic. She'd seen worse.

Her initial assessment over, she propped the picture at an angle and stood back a pace, taking it in fresh, purely as a portrait, a lifesize record of what someone had looked like in a time before photography. It was as if the artist had tried to freeze a reflection of the girl as she sat before the vanity mirror of her dresser.

The beautiful girl was posed in the center of the picture, her hands folded serenely before her. Her pale cheeks were soft and full with youth, her lips narrowed with a certain stoic acceptance. Dark brown hair had been pulled up into a coquettish coif, unsuccessfully attempting to age a girl who would have looked more natural in braids. Her blue eyes were gentle, unafraid, framed by black lashes and brows. A single enormous pearl hung from a narrow ribbon around her neck and a straight, thin row of lace topped the bodice of her light blue satin dress. Louisa de Plentagon.

Therese took another step back, standing shoulder to shoulder with Milo, and then she saw it. Her breath caught. From this distance, the pieces of the portrait— Louisa's features, the ribbon, the dress, the young woman's posture—merged together into one luminescent impression of innocence. She exhaled slowly, her gaze traveling over the portrait again and again, still not believing what she was really seeing. Purity, fluid grace. Not näiveté or ignorance, but true innocence. And the girl looked alive in a way that was uncanny. She had to put out her hand to believe that Louisa wasn't real.

"She went on to have fifteen children?" Therese asked.

"It doesn't seem possible, does it?"

She shook her head, still captivated by the sweetness in Louisa's expression.

"Can you restore her?" he asked.

She stepped close again and the innocence disappeared, leaving so many brushstrokes and spots of damage. It was like a magic door that could be seen only at a certain angle. She turned to see if Milo was aware of this trick of distance, but he was still gazing at the painting, a look of unveiled longing in his eyes that was so raw, it almost hurt her. Her heart turned a fraction in her chest.

There was a trick door to Milo too, she realized, and she had found it. Oh, Milo, she thought, as she sensed the core of loneliness in him. Was it his own innocence he longed for or someone else's?

When he looked at her, his expression shifted instantly to hide the vulnerability he'd unconsciously exposed.

"Well?" he demanded. "I asked if you could restore her."

"I told you I could even before I saw it," she said. "And I was right. I'll need a couple of things from the museum, but you have everything else I need."

He seemed pleased. "Then you could start now?"

She smiled. "Almost. Look here." She pointed to a faint seam at the top left of the canvas. "Before an artist begins, he or she constructs a wooden stretcher and stretches canvas over it tightly, as tight as a drum. Now they use staple guns to secure it, but back then they used nails." Carefully, she lifted the portrait to show him the back. "This canvas was removed from the original stretcher once, perhaps because it would have been easier to transport it that way. Bad idea, if you ask the painting. In any case, someone later constructed a new stretcher and stretched it on again." She showed him a fine row of old holes on the back side of the canvas, then the positions of the new nails.

"I see," he said, bringing his head near to hers. "And this line here means the new stretcher wasn't quite the right size?"

She could feel his breath just beside her ear, and his hand was inches in front of her face as he traced the line of nail holes. She couldn't help wondering what it would feel like to have his hand moving with the same carefulness along her own skin, and her heart picked up tempo.

"Or quite the right shape," she said slowly, her voice quiet. He turned to look at her, though she kept her gaze on the frame. "See how the canvas flaps slightly? And yet it's very fragile. To do this right," she went on, "I'll loosen the nails, tack the canvas on correctly, key out the corner with tiny wedges, making it about an eighth of an inch bigger, then secure the canvas again."

He stroked his hand farther along the frame, until she saw his thumb stop mere millimeters from her own hand.

"Is that hard?" he asked.

She turned her face slightly and there he was, inches away. It was as if they were sharing a secret, the secret of their closeness, their unspoken but mutual desire to see how close they could come before something sparked. She inhaled deeply and held her breath, waiting, and his thumb just grazed her own as he let go of the painting.

Deep inside, she felt a spark touch a match and flame. If Milo could make her feel this alive when he merely touched her hand, she thought, heaven help her if he ever kissed her. She laughed quietly, straightening away from him and setting the painting down. "It's not hard," she answered. "It just takes careful training."

She moved away from him and opened the box with the ultraviolet light. "Do you have a closet?"

He looked surprised. "It isn't very big."

"Just as long as it's big enough for the picture."

He opened a door beside the bathroom, exposing a small walk-in closet.

"That's perfect," Therese said. "Art conservators spend a lot of time in closets. Give me a hand here."

She and Milo carried the painting into the closet, resting it upright on a chair, then Therese connected the ultraviolet light to an extension cord. When she started to close herself in the closet with the painting, Milo stopped her.

"Can I see too?" he asked.

She felt her heart react strangely to the request, and she looked again at the small closet. There was hardly room for one person, let alone two.

"Just for a minute," he said. "Please?"

She swallowed hard and edged herself into one of the narrow corners. Flicking on the ultraviolet light, she looked back at him.

"Okay," she said.

Then he was in beside her and he closed the door. In the small space, she could hear him breathing and prayed he couldn't hear the beating of her own heart. If he moved at all, his right elbow would bump into her left arm. The ultraviolet light reflected strangely off his white shirt, making him glow a vibrant purple, while the painting shone with strange green fluorescence, practically concealing Louisa's form.

"Why is it all green?" Milo asked. His quiet voice was near in the muffling darkness.

"That's the natural resin varnish," she said, "a protective coating the artist put on when he was finished painting. And see these spots?" She pointed to areas that were black islands of darkness. "Someone overpainted here, covering the original paint with a new layer. I'm not the first person to treat this painting. Probably whoever restretched it also did the retouching."

She leaned nearer to a dark patch on Louisa's hand, gazing through the magnifying glass in the center of the UV light. The overpainted patch was so classic, she almost had the feeling she'd seen it before and then suddenly she had an odd sensation of memory, almost déjà vu. She gazed at it again, frowning.

"What is it?" Milo asked.

"Nothing," she assured him. The black area was a small clover shape over the left hand, Louisa's top hand, as she folded them on her lap.

Milo's elbow touched her arm as he tried to see around her, and Therese was instantly distracted. She nearly flinched.

"Is there something wrong?" he asked.

She straightened away from him, feeling the constriction of the tiny, dark space. He was so close, she could smell the dry cotton of his shirt and almost feel the heat emanating from his body. He turned his face to look at her, and she saw the green light reflecting faintly up from below, touching the angles of his handsome face. She gazed too long at the sensual curve of his lips and felt her chest tighten with vague alarm. Every nerve in her body tingled with sudden awareness of how close he was, how easy it would be to slide her fingers through the darkness and reach for him. She must be going mad, she thought.

"Could you open the door now?" she whispered.

She heard the knob click, then pure light flooded into the closet, half blinding her as her eyes adjusted. Milo backed out into the room, and Therese exhaled, feeling the release deep in her lungs.

Get . . . a . . . grip, she warned herself, but she couldn't bring herself to look at Milo. She was afraid he'd see how unsettled she'd been by his proximity.

She busied herself carrying the portrait out of the closet and Milo assisted her. She promised herself she'd finish with the ultraviolet light later, when she could occupy the closet alone.

"Why would someone cover over a place in a painting?" he asked.

"Lots of reasons," she said. "There have always been censors to paint out a family's coat of arms, or cover a saint's wounds, or simply add in a few key fig leaves. And there are practical reasons too. Suppose something was spilled or dropped on a painting. Without the right techniques, the average person couldn't get the stain off, but even a moderately good artist could paint over the place. At least the new paint wouldn't be as conspicuous as a wine stain. You said it was hung in a kitchen once, didn't you? That could account for it."

He was watching her closely. "I didn't say it was hung in a kitchen."

She was puzzled for only a moment. "I guess I just pictured it over one of those big stone fireplaces in a kitchen." She laughed. "You know, with boorish ale-drinking farmers or hunters hollering around a big table. It was all your talk of run-down mansions and wine cellars that got me going, I guess."

Milo didn't smile. "It did hang in a kitchen," he said. "Much as you described. That's where your father left it."

Therese felt a chill wrap around her heart. She pressed her lips together. "Are you suggesting my father told me that?"

"I don't know," Milo said. "It's possible. He might have told you a story about a painting like this."

She shook her head. "He was always telling me stories, millions of them. I was just a child then. They've all become a blur."

She could see something uncertain in Milo's eyes and tension in his jawline.

"Why is this restoration so important right now?" she asked. "Clearly it's gone neglected a long time."

He backed up slightly and considered her. She wondered if he ever gave a simple, unguarded answer, or if he always hoarded his thoughts. What secrets had forced him to practice such reserve? And why did she have the feeling he was about to lie?

"There's a woman who needs to see it and she can't wait," he said.

"Why not?"

"Because she's going blind."

Therese was genuinely surprised. "Why not show it to her the way it is?" she asked. "Can someone really go blind so rapidly?"

"Yes, they can." He turned away from her and began cleaning up the mess of the crate.

"Who is she?" Therese asked.

He kept cleaning while he spoke. "Her name's

Beatrice de Blanc. She's a friend of mine, a very important friend. And the painting rightly belongs to her."

"It's not yours?" Therese was more surprised than ever. "Do you have the right to authorize this restoration?"

He straightened and faced her squarely. "I do," he said, his voice cool. "Do you have any other impertinent questions?"

For a while there he'd almost seemed like other men, someone who could look unruly upon waking, someone who needed a shower and a shave, someone who would stand in a dark closet to see a UV light effect. Now his formal facade covered him again like a second layer of clothes, effectively distancing him from her. It was the raw man beneath that she wanted to emerge again. And he'd provided an opening she couldn't refuse.

"Actually, I do have another question," she said. "Are you married?"

His expression was unreadable. "No. Are you?"

She smiled, flashing her fingers before his face. "Do I look like I'm hiding a diamond?"

His face went strangely colorless, then he transferred his gaze to her bare fingers. When he looked back at her face, he'd recovered his composure.

"I find it hard to believe you don't have a boyfriend at least," he said.

She shrugged and dropped her gaze to the portrait on the table. "I was engaged once." She leaned forward so that her hips met the edge of the table. Pressing her hands to the small of her back, she stretched slightly to erase the tension of her memories. "My fiancé died. Since then I haven't had much taste for dating."

"I'm sorry," Milo said quietly.

She looked up, blinking him back into focus. "It's all right. It was seven, no, eight years ago now. Most of my Boston friends don't even know. What about you?"

He gave her an evasive smile. "I'm not the marrying type, I guess. No woman with any sense gets anywhere near me."

She found that hard to believe, especially considering how affected she had been by him in the closet. "Do you mean that once a woman gets close to you, she loses her mind?" she asked dryly.

He laughed, a low, resonant rumble. "Care to find out?"

She thought he was joking, but he moved nearer, then even nearer, until he stood so close, his sleeve nearly touched her own.

"We shouldn't have to stand in a closet to see what happens between us, Therese," he murmured.

She held her breath, steeling her senses against him, but when she glanced up at his face, his eyes held warmth and an intimate question.

Slowly, without breaking his gaze from hers, he reached up with a finger and traced the line of her jaw, from below her ear to the front of her chin, leaving her skin deliciously sensitized. It was the same careful, searching touch he'd used on the painting earlier, when she'd wished for a similar caress, only the effect was far more evocative than she'd ever imagined.

Therese held herself completely still, while a riot of emotions raced through her. His gaze dropped briefly to her lips, and she saw him compress his own lips, considering. Then he seemed to remember himself with an effort and stepped back. She searched his features and saw a hint of color in his tanned cheeks.

"I'd have to say," he drawled casually, "that's one experiment that backfired." He turned and strode over to his desk.

Not completely, she thought. Her lungs expanded as she began to breathe again, sharp, shallow breaths, as if she'd come up from underwater.

She cleared her throat. "I need to borrow a couple of tools from the museum."

He nodded and began shuffling papers on his desk. "That's fine. I need to stay with the painting."

She had thought he might offer her a ride or lunch or something. "You're serious?"

His eyebrow lifted. "Of course. This is a very important painting. It must be protected at all times."

She stared. "You don't intend to leave this apartment at all until the guard comes on Monday? How are you going to eat?"

"I'll order in pizza."

"You can't survive on pizza for three days. What about the food pyramid?" She pointed a knowing finger at him. "What about caffeine?"

He only shrugged.

She threw up her hands. "When did you eat last?"

He evaded her gaze, stuffing a hand into his jeans pocket. With that one defensive gesture, Therese was hooked. Her protective, maternal side went into high gear.

"Yesterday?" she prodded.

He ran a hand through his hair, looking suspiciously like a cornered schoolboy. "I slept yesterday."

"You haven't eaten since two days ago?" she asked. "And you expect me to go ahead and work while you're starving? Of all the self-destructive, obsessive, boneheaded people—"

"You left out 'bulldozer.' It was bulldozer the first time." His expression was deadly serious, but his eyes were laughing.

She reached for her coat, refusing to be beguiled. "You stay here and play guard dog. I'm going to get groceries."

TWO

In the grocery store, Therese eyed the Granny Smith apple in her hand, automatically checking the green skin for blemishes. She turned it over quickly with a twist of her wrist, dropped it in the bag, and reached for another.

If she didn't find a way to set some limits with Milo Dansforth, she was going to be in for some serious trouble. And she didn't have time for trouble, not with her work at the museum and an outside renovation to complete. For the first time in a long while, she remembered Josh, her fiancé, who had died of leukemia when she was in college. She could hardly remember his features anymore, but she remembered his laugh and his sweet, young kisses. She'd been young herself, living in another lifetime, on another planet: St. Paul, Minnesota. Her father was still alive then and her grandparents' home was as secure as the rock of Gibraltar. Only Josh's illness had clouded the horizon, and they had believed, right to the end, that he would pull through.

She sighed, putting a couple more apples in the bag.

So much for believing in the power of idealistic love. Now she'd met Milo, a man who seemed to have nothing to do with sweet romance, yet he'd already worked devastating magic on her senses. And he hadn't even kissed her.

But he had to kiss her eventually, she thought. *Had* to.

Her mind replayed the sight of him bare-chested, standing in his comfortable black sweatpants, his dark hair wild over his forehead. Ruddy cheeks, penetrating eyes. All he needed was for his mouth to smile a little more and he'd be . . . What? Perfect?

Get real, Therese, she told herself, picking out a can opener and a spatula.

He was way too rich for her, way too worldly for her, and way too cryptic.

She could get used to money, she mused, frowning at the spatula. And that worldliness was probably just a facade. Well, actually, she thought, beginning to doubt her own logic, the worldly sophistication was pretty convincing.

And cryptic?

That was a problem, she acknowledged. The man had a thousand protective masks. Like with Louisa. She'd seen the lonely longing in his eyes when she sprang his trick door. Unfortunately, it was that glimpse of inner loneliness that appealed to her most, even more than his physique.

And he did have one amazing body.

She sniffed at a bag of ground coffee, then tossed that in the cart too. No matter how attractive she found Milo, she wasn't going to let her heart get trampled. She'd lost too many of the people she loved for reasons beyond her control. But her heart was in her own control. She'd just have to be on her guard.

Milo opened the door for her when she got back and reached for the grocery bags. "You were gone for hours," he said.

She gave him an irritated look and loosened her scarf. After battling Brookline traffic, waiting for a parking spot at the grocery store, then enduring a twenty-minute wait in the checkout lane and a man who kept putting his items on the conveyor belt before she'd finished with hers, the last thing she needed was impatience.

"Such gratitude," she said. "I'm overwhelmed. Flowers and chocolates—you shouldn't have."

He gave an understanding smile. "I mean, thanks for the groceries. Are you a truffles woman or are M&M's good enough?"

She glanced up at him and had a flashing image of him holding a gilded box of chocolates, offering them all to her. She felt an inner twinge of response, and her irritation dissipated.

"Cake," she answered. "Rich devil's food cake with mousse frosting. Or cheesecake with that chocolate-cookie crust on the bottom. That kills me."

As Milo set the grocery bags on the counter, he appeared hungry for the first time. "Anything like that in here?"

She faked remorse. "Oh, I'm sorry! I thought you just wanted breakfast cereal and frozen food."

He looked at her suspiciously, until she grinned.

"You've got a mean streak, don't you?" he asked.

"It's a very small, malnourished mean streak," she said.

"I'd say it's thriving."

She laughed. "There's more in my car," she said, starting out. To her surprise, he followed her down the stairs. "Do you dare to leave the painting alone for forty-two seconds?"

"I can see the front of the building from here," he said, lifting the hatchback on her Toyota. Besides the groceries, she'd picked up a couple of saucepans, a box of ceramic dishes, and a coffee machine.

"Nice work," he said.

"Actually, I think I've been demoted. I've never even gotten a cup of coffee for any of my other bosses, and you've got me buying the whole machine."

"Hey, this wasn't my idea."

She laughed, hoisting two bags against her hips. "You didn't exactly beg me not to go. If I recall correctly, you began to drool and hallucinate when I suggested getting some food."

He took the remaining bags and slammed the hatchback closed. "You don't sound like you're too worried about job security."

"Go ahead, fire me," she said, leading the way up the stairs. "I'm overqualified for shopping duty, anyway."

She marched up the first landing of stairs and paused, looking back at him. Milo had stopped on the bottom step to rebalance his bags as the door closed and he looked up at her, a curious expression on his face. With the sunlight pouring in from the window behind him, he looked youthful, energetic, and something more. He looked surprised.

"What?" she asked.

"It's nothing," he said. "I'd just forgotten."

"Forgotten what?"

"What it's like to joke around. In Paris, everything . . . well, at least . . ." He started over. "All my friends there are older, more formal. Even the social situations have a different quality to them. This is—"

"Watch out," she said. "You're losing your apples."

His bag had tipped, and three of the Granny Smiths rolled onto the tiled floor, where bits of grit clung to them. He bent down to retrieve them and the other grocery bag began to split down the side. She set her own bags down on the landing and descended quickly to help.

In the small space, they reached for the fruit and nearly bumped into each other, green apples and sunlight and winter coats creating a kaleidoscope of color until Milo finally had his bags steady in his arms. Therese eyed him skeptically.

"I got it. No, really. I got it," he said.

But the top apple slipped again from his bag, and she reached out instinctively, catching it handily.

She smiled and looked up at him, suddenly aware of how close he was standing, of how warm and approachable he was with the fragrant scents of fruit and ground coffee rising from the bags in his arms. Her eyes were just on a level with his chin, and she could see a faint short scar in the dip of skin above his lips. She curled the apple near to herself and felt his gaze follow the motion before he met her eyes again. A twinge of shy pleasure tickled her, and she had a feeling he was also aware of the light energy, like the sunlight, that ran between them. Curiosity sank through her, and she shifted her gaze to his eyes.

He was doing it again, perusing her face with unwarranted intensity, as if she surprised him simply by existing. She could feel the heat rising in her cheeks.

"Nice catch," he murmured. He seemed completely indifferent to the awkward weight of the groceries in his arms.

Then he leaned nearer and gently kissed her lips. Therese felt the floor tip beneath her feet and locked her knees to keep from falling. It was the lightest of kisses, hardly more than a grazing of his lips against hers, yet he lingered an instant afterward, his breath mingling with hers while he gazed at her, waiting, curious.

It wasn't fair, she thought. How could he play with her when she wanted so much more?

Her own silent demand shocked her and she blushed furiously. Milo's small, knowing smile told her more clearly than any words could have that he'd seen exactly what she was thinking.

A buzzer sounded and someone began to enter the building. Therese pivoted quickly and preceded Milo up the stairs, grabbing her bags of groceries and trying to steady her heart. What was he thinking? She closed her eyes, waiting for him to come up behind her and let them in. When she opened her eyes again, he was holding the door open for her, politely waiting.

With a thud of disappointment, she realized he wasn't going to say anything about it, that this kiss was so casual to him, so unimportant, it didn't even warrant any awkwardness afterward.

I'm way out of my league, she thought. She walked purposefully over to the studio area and took off her coat, leaving him to deal with the groceries and other supplies.

In a moment, she had herself back in control and silently applauded herself for not doing anything ridiculously naïve, like throwing herself in his arms for a continuation of their embrace. Perhaps he was interested in a dalliance while he was here. Maybe that's what he was leading up to. She wished she knew more about his love life and how he conducted his affairs. He must have had lovers before, despite what he'd said about no woman with sense getting near him.

"How long have you lived in Paris?" she asked.

"Long enough to be spoiled by the coffee."

"How long is that? Fifteen minutes?"

He looked over his shoulder with a smile. "Twelve years," he said. "Not counting a few years in Cambridge and Florence. Do you travel much?"

"My dad used to. Every summer he used to take me to São Paulo to visit my mother's family, and then when I was in college, I studied in Madrid for a year." That was the year after Josh had died, when she'd badly needed a new place, new interests to help her through her loss. "Later, for restoration work, I lived in Paris for half a year. I like Boston, though. Especially in the spring."

"So your dad never took you to Romania?"

She watched him opening a can of soup, trying to appear casual. But she could tell he thought she knew something more about her father's work in Romania. He flipped the can opener around on its hinge, like an old-time gunfighter twirling his revolver, and waited for her response.

"I'll tell you if I remember something," she said quietly. "You don't have to pretend interest, just so you can pry."

He turned fully and she could see from his expression that she had guessed correctly. She was beginning to be able to read him, but it didn't make her any happier about what she saw. How much would he manipulate her if he could? she wondered.

He set down the can opener. "I'm not pretending the interest," he said.

She could feel the heat on her lips as his gaze lowered to them. All right, she thought. So it wasn't completely a farce. But what did he want?

His smile came again, more easily this time. "I tell you what," he said. "Why don't you ask me a few questions? Then we'll be even."

She smiled in return, then walked over to the stool set before the painting of Louisa. The windows were before her and to her left. Off to her right, she could hear Milo turning the gas heat on at the stove, the telltale clicking noise followed by the quick hiss of flame as the gas ignited.

"What actually do you do?" she asked.

"I'm an art dealer," he said, his voice sounding clearly in the open space. "I collect artworks, then resell them. I'm working on a book now, a sort of catalog of particular artworks in the private domain, with a bit of anecdotal lore thrown in."

"Does Louisa get mentioned?" she asked, looking down at the face of the lovely girl.

"Of course."

"And Louisa's owner?"

Milo's dark eyebrows lifted, but his gaze remained on the saucepan of soup.

"Beatrice. Yes, she's mentioned too."

Therese picked up a magnifying glass and leaned over the painting, but her mind was on Milo and the change in his voice when he said Beatrice's name. He said it as if she were a statue or a myth, the sort of person everyone was supposed to know about.

Beatrice, she thought. A Parisian woman who owned rare portraits. She tried to say "Beatrice" with a French accent under her breath, but it came out something like "Pay-a-treess?" and she swallowed a giggle.

"Do I get to meet her?" she asked.

"No."

Well, all right, she thought.

As if to make up for how abruptly he'd spoken, Milo glanced at her and gave half a shrug. "It so happens," he explained, "that Beatrice is Louisa's great-great-grand-daughter."

"Really?" Therese rested her elbow on the table and peered beyond the magnifying glass at him. "This is getting good."

He smiled, leaning a hip against the counter beside the burner. She couldn't get over the comfortable way his white shirt fit into the waistband of his pants, loose and snug at the same time, subtly revealing the clean lines of his masculine physique.

"It's a long story," he said, as if she might have second thoughts.

"It's a long afternoon," she replied.

He smiled over his pan, as if he were glad it would be long.

"Want some soup?" he asked.

"I ate already."

Looking up again, he gave her body a quick, critical

scan. She nearly winced at the impersonal nature of his assessment.

"You look like you could eat some more," he said.

"Is that a personal comment?" she asked.

He dipped a spoon in the pan and stirred, while his gaze slid again down her figure toward her boots, but this time it moved slowly, lingering appreciatively on each feminine curve. Therese blushed fiercely. By the time his eyes came back up to her face, she wanted to die of mortification, for his second appraisal had been anything but impersonal. She'd found another trick door.

"I guess that was a personal comment," he said, with the faintest hint of a drawl. "You want me to take it back?"

She bit inwardly on her lip, then the laughter rippled through her. She shook her head. "Why do I get the feeling you never take anything back?"

His slow, liquid grin did strange things to her knees. "Maybe because I don't."

Her heart beat a strange rhythm in her chest, and she looked down at the painting. She could hear his spoon clinking softly in the pan, then a smooth pouring sound.

"If I tell you about Beatrice," he said, "will you quit looking like you're going to pummel Louisa with that magnifying glass?"

She relaxed her grip on the glass. "That would be good," she said.

"All right." He pulled a chair over and sat opposite her, spooning soup out of a coffee mug while he talked.

"Beatrice loves beautiful things," he said, "and she has the money to pay for them. Her father left her a small fortune, and she made some very shrewd deals back when a million dollars meant something."

Fabulously wealthy, she thought. Orphan. "A million dollars is still a significant amount of money to some of us," she said.

Milo tilted his head to acknowledge this. "But she gives that much to charity without a thought. She does it anonymously. It's one of her quirks."

Therese laughed. "Some quirk. She sounds like a good person to know."

"She is. When I was released from my term in Romania, I had only one thing going for me, and it mattered a lot to Beatrice." He smiled. "I had worked with your father."

Surprised, Therese looked up from the painting. "You mean my dad knew Beatrice?"

Milo glanced expressively at the ceiling. "Did he ever. I think he knew everyone who ever had any interest in art. During the time he was in Romania, technically as a scholar, he recovered more than two dozen French paintings and returned them, for a modest commission, to the original owners or their descendants. You know about the Hermitage in St. Petersburg, don't you?"

She nodded. What art historian didn't? Aside from the vast collection legitimately housed there, countless paintings that Hitler's men had stolen had also ended up in the Russian museum, where they reportedly waited in storage—Matisse, Gauguin, an endless list of Impressionist masters.

"My father had nothing to do with the Hermitage," Therese said.

"Of course not," said Milo. "But there are stolen

paintings similarly hidden in other vaults in Eastern Europe, and your father seemed to know about several of them. Beatrice heard about your father. She wanted him to recover her family portrait and he agreed to do what he could."

Therese shook her head, incredulous. "But that must have been nearly impossible!"

Milo smiled over his mug. "If anybody could do it, Harry could. And he did try. But then, after he and I got caught in that basement, he dropped off the map. I know later Beatrice tried to get him to return for her portrait, but he was one of the few people who could say no to her and he did."

His voice had lowered, and she could see his thoughts had taken a darker turn. She wondered if Milo had ever needed to say no to Beatrice.

He walked back to the kitchenette and set his mug in the sink. Then he turned on the tap and reached for the dishwashing liquid.

She took a big breath and leaned back over the painting. "Where was your family during all this?" she asked over the noise of the water. "Didn't your parents get involved when you were arrested?"

"What's that?"

"What about your family?" she repeated.

He shut off the water and talked as he washed up.

"We moved to Romania when I was ten, and like your father, my parents were scholars at the university. I always think of them eating pears and reading books out loud. They'd get so excited, they'd read out loud to each other at the same time, and it seemed they could listen and talk simultaneously. They'd always end up laughing, and hugging, and hugging me too. I thought they were crazy. All I wanted to do was skip school and play soccer."

Therese laughed. "What happened? Where are they now?"

Milo reached for a dishtowel and dried his hands, inspecting each digit with unnecessary concentration. "They were killed in a fire. It was an electrical fire at one of their friends' houses, where they'd gone for dinner."

She sucked in a breath. "That's awful."

Milo inhaled deeply, then squinted toward the windows. His tone was low, as if the facts took the color out of his voice. "My life changed completely. There was no one back in the States to come home to and no relatives in Romania. The school took me in as a boarder, but I resented being a charity case. I started skipping, coming back only for dinner and a place to sleep. The director did not appreciate my attitude."

He shook his head. "Suffice it to say, I was well on my way to self-destructing. Then, one day, outside an art gallery, I ran into your father. He'd been an acquaintance of my parents', not even a friend really. But he knew they'd died and he took me to dinner. He talked some sense into me and let me ball my eyes out. He paid my tuition so that I wouldn't have to feel like I was a charity pupil, on the conditions that I stay through graduation and pay him back eventually."

Therese wasn't surprised. "That sounds like my dad."

"I'd have done anything for Harry," Milo said, with a slight, wry smile. "But he didn't want me hanging around. Then I heard something from one of my soccer buddies that I thought might be useful to Harry for his art dealings. It was. And he began to let me help him a

little, with translating, with maps, but nothing dangerous."

"Until the night in the basement?" Therese guessed.

Milo had folded the dishtowel into a compact roll.
Now he set it down on the counter and crossed to the
studio area. She could see he didn't blame her father for
causing him to be jailed, but she felt bad for him just the
same.

"Until that night," he agreed. "They called it 'detain-
ment,' and it wasn't so bad. I was a foreigner, after all, and
a minor. They pretty much just kept me running errands
for them so that I wouldn't get into worse trouble. And
they taught me chess." He laughed, gesturing to the living area, where the chess set was still set up on the small
table.

"And my father? Didn't he try to get you out?"

"He did what he could, but his own record wasn't
exactly beyond suspicion. And he was back in the States
by then."

She knew there had to be more to it.

She tried to imagine Milo after three years of "detain-
ment," no formal education, no resources, no family. It
couldn't have been easy. That must be where he'd learned
his wariness, acquired the edge of bitterness that surfaced
sometimes. No wonder he seemed so honed, so driven.
She sat up straighter on her stool, hitching her toes on
the rungs.

"What happened to you once you got out?" she asked

He exhaled heavily and crossed over to the windows,
where she watched him gaze down at the traffic.

"I moved to Paris and was earning money for school. I
applied for a scholarship that Beatrice sponsored, and

once she met me for an interview, she was like a fairy godmother. I couldn't believe my luck, but, of course, it was all because she'd put me together with Harry. She and her daughter gave me a place to go to for holidays. When I wanted to start my first art gallery, she financed my startup and sent all her wealthy friends to the gallery. She saved me a decade of struggle, any way you look at it. Have you heard of the Galleries Alvina?"

Therese smiled, pleased by a memory. "There was a Gallerie Alvina on the rue du Bac when I was in Paris. I used to walk past it every day on my way home from work." Her eyes grew wide as comprehension dawned. "That's your gallery?"

He nodded.

Her mind skipped ahead. He'd said "galleries," plural. Good God, she thought. There were half a dozen Galleries Alvina in Europe, known especially for their support of controversial new artists. Her breath came out in a quiet whistle. Did Milo own all of them? He must.

"I'm impressed," she said.

He shrugged off her admiration. "That first one turned out well, thanks to Beatrice. And the only thing she's ever asked in return is that I do whatever possible to recover her picture, the very picture I'd stashed with your father in the wine cellar. I wanted to do it for her. It was the ultimate challenge, and all I had to do was wait until memories faded and I could go back to Romania." He pivoted to face her. "The whole world changed over there, and I got my chance two months ago."

"Beatrice must have been overjoyed when you recovered the painting."

"She was. She can't wait to see it."

Therese frowned. "You said before that she's going blind."

He nodded. "That's right. She has creeping glaucoma. She has some drops she puts in seven times a day, but she started them too late."

"But then why don't you take the painting to her?" Therese asked, puzzled. "It's still clear enough to see."

"No," he said firmly. "It needs to be cleaned and restored first. That's where you come in."

Therese sat up and clutched the handle of the magnifying glass hard in her fist. She took a long look at his face, trying to gauge how far she could go.

"So are Beatrice and her daughter like family to you now?"

He squinted slightly, but he held her gaze. "No," he answered. "I respect Beatrice enormously, and I'm grateful to her. And I'd be loyal to her even if it cost everything I own, but they're not like family to me. It's hard to explain." He frowned, as if he weren't used to discussing his private life. "These are personal questions, I think."

Her gaze faltered, and she felt the heat of a blush rising up her neck. She'd been so engrossed by his story, she'd forgotten that she hardly knew him, that he'd given her no right to question him about his intimate past.

"Should I take them back?" she asked softly, echoing his earlier response.

He walked close to her, until he was just an arm's length away, then he reached forward and picked up the end of her black braid. Startled, she glanced at his fingers and saw that the blue string had come undone. He was gently, carefully, tying it for her.

"I've been wanting to do that for the last half hour," he said.

She twined her fingers together around the magnifying glass, holding perfectly still, while a riot of awareness circled in her gut. Her cheeks felt light and hot at the same time as she watched him adjust each loop to the same size.

"You're very precise," she murmured.

He smoothed his thumb over the end of the braid. "Why do you care about my family?"

Her gaze bolted up to his. "I don't know," she answered honestly. "It says so much about a person, I guess."

He tilted his face, watching her. "So you ask everyone you meet about their families?"

She shook her head, swallowing hard.

"Just me?"

She could see his gaze shift downward to her lips and the liquid heat of desire coursed through her. *Kiss me*, she thought.

He moved tantalizingly near, his eyes searching hers, until she felt the feather touch of his breath upon her mouth. He gave her braid the slightest pull, and she leaned into him, lifting her lips to his and moaning with relief and desire as finally he kissed her.

Where his first kiss had been brief, almost casual, this one plumbed straight through to the need that beckoned in her soul. His lips were incredibly sensual and warm, demanding yet intimately attuned to her response. Therese responded hungrily, giving in to the attraction that had pulled her toward him ever since that first day in A.K.'s office. She lifted one hand behind his neck and felt him steel his arms around her, pulling her off the stool until his hard chest was warm against her own. The tip of his tongue grazed the edge of her lip and she melted into him, stretching up on her toes to increase the intimacy of their embrace.

When his lips left hers at last, his eyes were smoldering with dark passion and the watchful curiosity she was beginning to expect. That curiosity seemed to say as much about him as it did about her, as if he was surprised by the response she evoked in him as much as he was delighted by her sensuality.

She smiled slowly, feeling the new, weighty ease in her lips, and he shifted his arms to cradle her loosely before him.

"I'm glad we finally got that part cleared up," he said, his voice warm with mirth.

"What part?"

"That part about how much I want to kiss you and how much you want to kiss me too."

She blushed again. "Oh. That part." She cleared her throat.

"I think I'm looking forward to having you work here every night," he said. "Do you think you can take a break occasionally so we can review that part again?"

She felt a sinking of uncertainty. She hadn't been thinking clearly. It was going to be awful trying to concentrate with Milo just across the room. She could have kicked herself. It was bad to mix business with romance. She'd seen it wreak havoc for her friends at the museum, yet here she was getting into it herself.

She felt for her braid, shifting slightly. Instantly he released her and stepped back half a pace.

"Therese?" he asked. His watchful expression had returned full force, increasing her confusion.

"Maybe this wasn't the greatest idea, Milo."

"I'd say it was more down the line of inevitable," he said quietly.

She shook her head and walked rapidly around the table to hide her agitation. It didn't work.

"Don't apologize, whatever you do," he said.

"I wasn't going to apologize."

He arched an eyebrow, clearly skeptical. "Then what?"

"Listen, Mr. Dansforth," she said. "This is not Tom Sawyer with the whitewash, but it isn't the Sistine Chapel either. It's somewhere in between. I need to be able to concentrate during the next two months, and you pose—" She stopped, blushing more furiously than ever. "You pose a considerable distraction."

He crossed his arms over his chest, apparently amused. "What do you propose I do about it?"

She'd never been in this position before. All it had been was a kiss! Why was she carrying on? But all she had to do was take one good look at him and she knew it had been more than a simple kiss. His smoky gaze was half taunting, half knowing, and one hundred percent devastating. He was a threat to her total way of life.

"You've explained that this restoration is of vital importance," she said. "Fine. If you want me to work my best, there are a few rules we should establish." She evaded his gaze, trying to remember some of the guidelines she had at the museum. "Don't expect me to answer phone calls or the door when I'm working. I usually don't even hear them. Don't try to interrupt me if I'm concentrating because I'll bite your head off. And finally, make sure there's always enough coffee around."

A glimmer of amusement lit his gray eyes. "And I thought that coffeemaker was for me. Anything else?"

She paced to the windows and turned her back on them, taking in the whole room—the sunlight, the waiting portrait, Milo's work area, the kitchenette, and that maddening bed. She breathed in deeply, then exhaled.

This was going to be the most difficult project she'd had in a long time, made more arduous because of the late hours when she was already overworked. She could feel herself rising to the pressure, setting the gears that would drive her from within. Only one thing could sabotage the whole thing. Milo waited, his head cocked. She looked him straight in the eye.

"These personal questions," she said. "I think we'd better try to avoid them. And make sure you don't answer the door in your sweatpants again."

His eyes gleamed with pleased amusement, but she had no assurance he'd accept her rules. He surveyed her with a slow, leisurely look.

"The last thing I want is to slow down the restoration," he said. "I'll give your rules a trial period, out of deference to your professional expertise. But if I don't think they're working, if I decide some other rules might work better, then I warn you, I may answer the door in whatever I please."

THREE

For the next three weeks Milo met her nightly at the museum, drove her to the studio, waited until she was too tired to work, then, after one of the security guards he'd hired arrived, he drove her home. As the exhaustion began to catch up with her, she yearned for a good, long soak in her tub, but there was hardly time for her to keep herself fed, let alone relax. She felt as tensely overstretched as a tightrope and as tired as a marathon runner on an isolated back stretch. But it was worth it. The progress on Louisa was steady and satisfying, and her routine with Milo was becoming so ingrained in her, so indispensable a part of her day, she could hardly imagine a time when he wasn't in her life.

True to his word, he steered away from personal questions and never once did he try to kiss her, but that didn't mean he didn't watch her. Many times she looked up from her work to find him sitting at his computer, where he answered his E-mail and worked on his art book. If he wasn't looking at her already, he would instantly sense her gaze and turn to smile at her. "Ready for coffee?" he'd ask.

Though she always felt the pull of attraction, she forced herself to ignore it. In answer to his question she would smile and shake her head, returning to her work. Only later would she realize he'd put a cup of coffee and a pile of M&M's beside her elbow.

She was touched by his small, supportive efforts, but she felt an increasing uneasiness about him as well. He was too calm, too genial, as if he'd put the real Milo on hold. She knew the passionate, darker side of him was there beneath the surface, but he kept it so firmly under control that she was reminded of a simmering volcano. A Hawaiian volcano, with hibiscus bushes and mango trees growing on its slopes, while turbulence converged beneath, preparing for a molten burst of fire.

And some crazy, unidentifiable change was happening inside her too. She knew it from her sleeplessness and from the half dreams that trailed after her in the morning. Though Louisa's face filled her vision during her waking hours, it was Milo's face that crowded in when she attempted to sleep. Try as she might, she couldn't ignore the fact that she missed the fiery, driven, passionate man who'd kissed her, and she couldn't ignore her disappointment that he could so easily achieve a neutral demeanor with her.

You asked *for the neutral man, idiot*, she reminded herself.

The neutral man who would do nothing to interfere with her speedy restoration of Louisa.

Was she imagining the unacknowledged chemistry she still felt between them?

One night, when she glanced up at the window, she saw Milo's reflection clearly in the pane of glass and allowed herself a real look at him: the angle of his head as he leaned his chin on his fist, his eyes squinting in concentration at his computer screen. His dark hair gleamed in the lamplight, and his white shirtsleeve puckered where his elbow was bent, subtly outlining the muscles beneath. In the reflection he was power and intelligence and intensity all rolled into one, and even when he wasn't looking at her, even when his concentration was focused on the computer before him, she felt a magnetic pull to him that lifted her half out of her seat.

He heard her movement and turned toward her, but she dropped her gaze from his reflection before he could see it. She held still for a full minute, sensing his gaze upon her, thinking he was going to speak, but finally he just looked back at the computer.

"This isn't going to work much longer," she mumbled, trying to calm the churning heat in her belly.

The next night, as she was waiting for Milo to pick her up, Therese could feel her nervousness coming on again. Could three weeks of working beside someone in silent tandem mean something? Was he exerting some kind of water-on-the-rock method of influence on her, waiting her out? But what, exactly, did he want from her?

Was it what she wanted from him? *No, Therese. Stop.* But her deeper thoughts took a devious turn all on their own, and she felt the pull of dread and desire that always attacked her when she knew she'd see him soon.

His car pulled up before the museum, and she dashed

out, hunching against the steady rain, and practically dove into his car. She fingered her wet bangs back from her forehead, gasping with quick laughter. The rain made a pleasing, clattering noise on the roof and windshield, adding to her pleasure of starting another night with Milo, but his face in the dim light looked serious. His hands firmly gripped the steering wheel, but he made no effort to steer the car into traffic, and she sensed immediately that the hibiscus and mangoes were in for a shock.

"Where's that cheery hello?" she asked.

"Did you have dinner?" he asked in return.

Startled, she thought for a moment. "No," she said slowly. She wiped her wet fingers on the hem of her coat. "But I had a couple of muffins left over from a reception this morning."

His eyebrows drew together, as if that was what he'd expected. "Tell me something, Therese." His voice was suspiciously mild. "Have you been skipping dinner these last three weeks?"

She felt an instant of guilty panic in her gut, then annoyance. "Do I look like a dope to you?" she asked.

"You didn't answer the question."

She snapped her seat belt on sharply. "You're the one who didn't eat for two days when you first got here."

"That's because I couldn't leave the painting."

"Well, what do you think I've been working on?"

He frowned at the windshield, then turned to face her.

"I never thought I'd say this to anyone," he said, "but you work even more than I do. You're exhausted and half starved, and all that's left of your face are the rings under your eyes. When are you going to take a break?"

She was floored, absolutely stunned. Half of her thought that he was incredibly sweet to be concerned, but the independent half of her was outraged that he was presuming to criticize her. She gave him ten seconds to apologize, but he merely sat there, his face a stony mask of superiority.

"Who asked for your opinion?" she snapped.

He braced a fist against the steering wheel. "Would you just answer me?"

"If it's of any interest to you," she said, "I'm going to take Saturday morning off. And I have a snack late, when I get home. What is this, Milo? I thought you were in a hurry for this restoration."

"I am," he agreed. "But I don't want any corpses chalked up to the process."

"Ha!" She laughed at the insult. "I'm hardly a corpse."

"Have you looked at yourself lately?"

"Oh, very nice. Give a lady a compliment, why don't you."

He looked utterly exasperated. "Don't you ever take care of yourself?"

She shrugged, looking out the rain-soaked windshield.

A tense silence stretched out, accentuated by the noise of the rain and an occasional honk from the traffic on Huntington. Therese could smell the faint trace of mint and soap that she always associated with him, and she shoved her hands under her legs to stop them from fidgeting conspicuously. She refused to give him the satisfaction of an answer.

"And this idiotic no-personal-questions rule," he added, his voice low. "That's got to go."

She bit her lower lip, feeling a prickling of alarm. "I don't need this right now, Milo," she said. But her strong words were betrayed by her voice, which came out with husky vulnerability. She closed her eyes, praying he'd let it drop, knowing with a rush of adrenaline that he wouldn't.

She felt the lightest touch on her cheek and turned. He'd reached his hand to her, and the gentle pressure of his warm finger along her jaw kept her face turned to his until she looked up at him. Her skin became startlingly alive to his caress, almost as if it burned her, but she couldn't draw away.

"You may not need this, Therese," he said, "but I do."

Then his lips were against hers, kissing her with a honeyed warmth that pulled her surely against him. She was incapable of thought, let alone resistance, and she matched his every subtle move until her lips clung to his with agonizing intensity. The longing she had tried to ignore rose to the surface in a surging wave, pouring molten heat through her body, making it simultaneously taut and liquid with want.

When she moaned deep in her throat, he withdrew slightly, his gaze boring into her as she opened her eyes.

"You're taking the evening off," he said.

She swallowed hard, fighting to regain control of her scattered feelings. The first rational thought to penetrate was that he didn't want her at the studio with him, and a knot of hurt tightened inside her.

"Is that an order?" she asked.

He glanced away from her, a muscle working in his jaw as if he was trying to maintain his control.

"Would you take an order from me if I gave it?" he asked.

She forced a laugh. "No. Probably not."

He looked back at her, his eyes serious and warm. "What if I said please?"

A crushing hopefulness sent her heart spinning in a new direction. Don't start being concerned about me, she wanted to tell him. If he kissed her like a dream *and* said he was concerned about her, she was going to be in terrible trouble.

"Can we go now?" she asked.

He lifted a hand and ran it back through his dark hair. "You are the most obstinate, uncooperative, obsessive person I've ever met," he said, visibly frustrated.

She issued a sharp laugh. "That's great, coming from you. You've only focused your entire adult life on recovering one painting."

"And you are not working on it tonight."

She rolled her eyes. "Because you've decided I need a lesson in moderation," she said, a mimicking tone creeping into her voice. "And certain kisses and personal questions have nothing to do with it. This is an order from the boss."

He pressed his lips together into a tight line. "Correct."

But she'd seen. Kisses and personal questions had everything to do with his concern, and a lesson in moderation was the last thing he wanted to teach her. "Liar," she said softly.

He seemed to freeze. But then he turned the car key

with a quick, savage motion and revved the engine. She shook her head as he gave the steering wheel a half spin and pulled the car into the traffic.

"Very macho," she said. "Just don't get us killed while you're at it."

He didn't answer. He drove like a taxi driver, swift and confident, cutting so deftly around other cars that they didn't even honk at him. The streetlights, red tail-lights, and glowing windows passed with amazing speed. Therese was not impressed. She herself could handle Boston traffic with one eye closed. But she was well aware that he was telling her something about how angry he felt, and she began to regret calling him a liar. She had only needed an outlet for the energy she felt between them, had only meant to let him know she couldn't be fooled, but obviously she'd hit a nerve.

At the next corner, he stopped in front of a Chinese restaurant and pulled up the emergency brake with a creaking sound.

"Wait here," he said tersely.

His door slammed behind him, and he disappeared into the restaurant. Through the rain, Therese saw an array of authentic Chinese characters set vertically down each side of the door in bright yellow fluorescent lights. WOK TALL, a sign read at the top. She hardly had time to smile at the pun before Milo strode out the door. He thrust a steamy, fragrant paper bag onto her lap and started the car again.

"Did you steal it off someone's plate or just put a gun to the cook's head?" she asked.

"I called ahead," he said dryly. "That usually works for me."

She mouthed a silent "Oh" while he pulled back into traffic, then she chuckled to herself.

He shot her a quick glance, but she pretended she didn't notice.

The interior of the car began to fill with the rich scents of ginger and soy sauce, and Therese breathed deeply. At least he would feed her before he took her home, she thought. The evening wouldn't be a total loss. The bag was hot on her lap, and she could feel the weighty, square boxes inside. Milo was driving more slowly. The rushing tires on the wet road had a soporific effect on her, and she let her eyes close, just for a moment. Tension that had compounded in her shoulders for weeks began to ease, and she stretched her neck back, getting comfortable against the headrest.

Maybe she was just a little bit tired, she thought. Too tired to sustain any more arguments with Milo. How nice it would be if they could just be friends for once.

He pulled the car into a parking spot and cut the engine. With an effort, she opened her eyes. Milo was already out of the car and a second later he opened her door for her. When he took the paper bag of food from her, it left a sudden cool space against her lap.

"Where are we?" she asked, surprised not to recognize the street they were on.

"Out you come, sleepyhead," he said.

She couldn't tell if he was amused or annoyed, but she took off her seat belt and stepped out into the drizzle.

He slammed her door, then half sheltered her with his body as they hurried to the doorway of a neat brick house. The wind blew them into the foyer, then the door blew shut with a smack.

Milo reached for the lights, and she had a quick impression of a small but expensively furnished living room through one doorway, a library lined with books through another. She turned rounded eyes to Milo.

He was shucking his coat, much as he had when she first met him, only this time those magnificent shoulders were in tantalizing proximity to her. He was casually dressed, black slacks, a green cotton shirt, and a plain black tie, and her cold fingers longed to touch him. She knew instantly that this was his home and that no one else was there.

He reached for her coat. "Unless you don't intend to stay," he said dryly, when she hesitated.

She quickly took off her coat.

"Is this where you're living?" she asked, glancing around again. A small curious table in the hallway held a tray of letters and a list that looked like a maid had left it.

"When I'm not at the studio," he said.

He led her around a corner, past the kitchen, around another corner, up a few stairs, and into a wide, unexpectedly fragrant room. She paused by the doorway and watched as he turned on the lights.

A nighttime solarium, filled with plants, small trees, and flowering gardenias filled her senses. Rain poured onto the sloped glass ceiling above and dripped down the old-fashioned small-paned windows, while garden lights, cleverly hidden among the plants, sent shadows of leaves up into the corners. A grouping of two small couches, chairs, and a table had been arranged to one side, leaving an open area on the plush patterned carpet that covered most of the green tiled floor. In the center of the carpet, arranged with half a dozen throw pillows, was a red-checked blanket. Laid out on it were dark blue china plates, a bowl of watermelon slices, a basket with a small ice bucket inside it, a bottle of wine cozied inside that, and two wineglasses. An indoor picnic.

Milo walked farther in and set the bag of Chinese food on the low table beside the picnic area.

"You did this?" she asked. She couldn't believe it.

"It wasn't elves," he said. Then, with a great show of getting comfortable, he sat down on the blanket, stretched out his legs, and leaned back against a couple of the cushions.

She couldn't help but observe how strong he looked, how invitingly masculine in his deep green shirt. With his dark hair and intense, flashing eyes, he was like a wild thing from a mountainside brought in among the tame, carefully arranged greenery of the solarium.

"Are you coming in?" The smile he gave her was as warmly welcoming as a summer morning. And here it was, a rainy winter night.

"Why didn't you just say you wanted to invite me on a picnic?" she asked, stepping forward. "Were you afraid I wouldn't come?"

"Something like that." His glance darted to the side, then he smiled and looked back at her. "But then you called me a liar and I knew we were off to a good start."

She laughed. "What do you consider a bad start?"

He tipped his face slightly, watching her. "I don't know."

She slipped out of her shoes, then sat on the far corner of the blanket. She tucked her feet under her, folded her skirt around her long legs, and reached for a pillow to set at the base of her back. By bracing the pillow against a low stone wall that bordered the plants, she could sit upright and still relax.

He watched her closely the whole time, and she resettled her legs, checking her skirt to be sure that she wasn't giving him an inappropriate view.

"What is this place?" she asked. "You said you lived in Paris."

He shrugged and uncorked the wine, then poured a glass. "I like to be comfortable, and I knew I'd be here for a while. It's a rental, but I'm thinking about buying it. You like it?" He handed her the glass.

She nodded, remembering the intimate glimpses she'd had of the other rooms. If the bedrooms were as nice, it would be a perfect city home. And big, compared with other places she'd seen. It must cost a fortune, and it must echo with emptiness when no one was home.

"It's a lot of space for a single guy," she said.

When his eyes flicked up to hers and held, curious, she began to feel uncomfortable. Of course Milo could afford huge homes.

"I'm sorry," she said. "It's just that the men I know . . ." Her cheeks flamed with color, and she stopped.

Milo's eyes narrowed slightly and he held his glass before his face, watching her over the rim. "Yes, what about the men you know?"

She shook her head.

"They have smaller homes?" he asked. "You've seen many?"

She stared down into the trembling red liquid in her wineglass. His question resonated between them, taking on an overtone that increased her embarrassment. It was almost as if he wasn't aware that she was a virgin. She'd only meant that the men she knew got married before they bought family-sized homes. But she couldn't say that, not to Milo. Not now. Not when he knew she wasn't big on dates but still chose to make fun of the fact. Or maybe he'd forgotten she'd told him she didn't date much, not after Josh.

She wished she could respond to his comment with a teasing reply of her own, but she couldn't. Finally she managed a laugh. "I think this qualifies as a bad start," she said with dry honesty.

For one instant Milo froze, then he set his wineglass down and raked both hands through his hair.

"I'm sorry," he said quickly, his voice low. "I never meant to imply . . ."

He stopped, and she looked up hesitantly to see the concern etched on his features. Her heart did a neat little dive in her chest.

He inhaled deeply. "All I've wanted, all day," he said, "was to see you here having a picnic with me. It turned out I had to kidnap you and now I've made you unhappy."

A melting of pain spread through her, and she looked into his face, searching his eyes. He was so close, so intense. It was impossible to compare Milo Dansforth in any way to the men she'd known. That was her problem. While she was familiar with graduate students and artists and museum curators and unpretentious friends from the Midwest, he was Milo Dansforth, international art dealer. But she kept forgetting his status because he seemed so real to her. His lips were closed in a narrow line, and he looked almost grim. There was so much about him that she didn't know, she thought. And yet she wanted to. Why was that?

"Never unhappy," she said. "Just prepared to retaliate."

He smiled a slow, cautious smile, seeming to relax slightly. "I think I've already had a taste of your retaliation," he said. "Nobody's called me a liar since third grade."

"Why not?"

He thunked a fist against his chest, as if wounded, and winced. "Ouch," he said.

She laughed. "I mean, did you start telling the truth or did you beat somebody up so he was too scared to call you a liar another time?"

"What do you think?" he asked.

She let her gaze drift down over his arms and body, as if she could read the answer there. His shirt spread smoothly along his broad shoulders, and he looked warm, as if he had an extra source of heating energy inside. Slowly, her fingers began to tingle, anticipating what he would feel like if she could just touch those shoulders, just glide her palm up his sleeve and feel the warmth where his collar met his neck.

She swallowed hard, unable to bring her gaze all the way up to meet his eyes. "I think you began telling the truth," she said. Her voice was quiet, barely audible above the subdued pattering of the rain.

He remained silent until she had to look up at him. His eyebrows were lifted slightly, as if he hadn't expected her answer.

Maybe he thought she regretted calling him a liar. Maybe she did.

Caragh M. O'Brien

70

"You give me more credit than I deserve," he said. He shifted his focus to the bag of Chinese food. "Are you hungry?"

For what? she thought, but said only, "Sure."

"You want chopsticks or a fork?"

"Fork." She was keenly aware that the atmosphere had shifted, bringing them into safer territory with the pragmatic issue of food.

He handed her a plate heaped with rice and Chinese food. It smelled so delicious, it made her dizzy, and barely waiting until she saw Milo had served himself, she began to scarf down her dinner. She didn't pause, didn't look up until it was all gone, then she eyed Milo's plate with longing. He'd hardly eaten anything. His chopsticks were suspended over his plate, not even moving.

She looked over at the white cardboard boxes, but she could see by the way they were tilted that they were empty.

Milo began to chuckle.

"What?" she said defensively.

"Take mine," he said, offering his plate. The blue china was temptingly heaped, and she still felt positively starved.

"What if you have cooties or something?" she asked.

"Bit late for that, isn't it?"

She looked up at him, saw his significant glance at her lips, and blushed again. Shifting slightly, she repositioned herself against her pillow, then reached for his plate. His fingers just skimmed hers as he released it, and she felt a prickling in her belly that had nothing to do with dinner.

"Thanks," she murmured.

"My pleasure," he said.

And she could tell he did take pleasure in it, watching her every mouthful in a way that made her acutely self-conscious, but not nervous. She caught the last few grains of rice in the tines of her fork, then paused. "You're sure you don't want any more?"

He chuckled. "Glutton."

She smiled with satisfaction behind her napkin as she wiped her lips. "I really should eat more regularly."

"Now you say so."

She laughed. "Are there any fortune cookies?"

"I think so." He glanced down into the white bag and offered her one.

She cracked hers in two, pulled out the tiny slip of paper, and quickly rolled it into a ball. Milo stopped her just as she was about to pop it in her mouth.

"What are you doing?" he demanded.

"Eating my fortune."

"You can't do that."

She held the tiny white ball suspended between her thumb and forefinger. "Why not?"

"Aren't you going to read it?"

"It's bad luck."

He laughed. "Let me see it."

She shook her head. "No. If you read it, it might come true."

He held his hand toward her, palm up. "If I follow your superstitious logic, you eat your fortune so you won't know what it is and it won't come true."

She nodded.

"What if I read it and never tell you what it says?" he asked.

"I don't know," she said dubiously. "I always eat it. My dad always ate his."

"I promise I won't tell you what it says," he said, reaching closer.

She wavered, reluctant to surrender the tiny coil of paper.

"Will you give me yours?" she asked.

"Sure." He handed it over and she fingered his slip of paper, not reading it. Slowly, as if she were somehow conferring a great power upon him, she handed him her fortune.

He straightened it, then folded it once and slipped it in the breast pocket of his shirt.

She licked her lips. "You didn't read it."

"I will later."

Therese didn't know what to do with his fortune. She automatically rolled it into a tiny coil and folded it into her palm while she slowly ate the brittle pieces of her sweet cookie.

"Can I ask you something?" he said.

She felt the adrenaline of anticipation start in her gut. "A personal question?"

He didn't answer immediately but poured a stream of red wine into her glass. Then he refilled his own while she waited, watching the concentration on his features. She could read him better now, she realized. Where before he'd been inscrutable, now she could recognize the subtle differences of his expressions: annoyance had lowered eyebrows and a tenseness around his lips; concern for her was accompanied by a sort of lost space deep in his eyes. At the moment his deliberate hesitation revealed he cared deeply about something and was struggling for the right words.

His voice was low and warm when he finally spoke. "Your father taught you your fortune cookie trick," he said. "He taught me a lot too, a long time ago. But I don't know much about his last ten years or how he died. I wish you'd tell me about him."

"Ah," she said slowly. Her gaze shifted sideways, out the window, to where the rain was lost against the night. She had been so unhappy when her father and grandparents were killed, yet she'd come far in her grieving. She felt closer to her father now that she was working on Milo's project, as if his spirit were near, guiding her, and it didn't hurt her as much to remember him.

"He and my grandparents were on a trip out west when they were all killed. I was in my last year of college at the time. But I don't understand, Milo. I thought you and my father were friends."

He smiled uneasily. "After I left Romania, I called him, but when he heard Beatrice had taken me on, he became very remote. He was still angry at her and he thought I was making a mistake. We talked only a half a dozen times after that, and our conversations were always strained. He couldn't hide his disapproval, even when I paid back my debt to him. I think I'd disappointed him."

Therese was surprised. "You never told me this," she said.

He smiled, lifting his hand apologetically. "I didn't think it would help persuade you to take on the restoration."

Watching him, seeing the wariness in his eyes, she felt cheated somehow, manipulated. A small, warning voice inside her whispered cold words of caution. If he wasn't an actual liar, he was very deft with the skill of omission.

"You were right," she said.

"Don't be angry with me," Milo said. "Your father was wrong about Beatrice. He had to be. I could only be loyal to one of them and I had to pick her."

Therese frowned, looking down at her blue skirt. All her pleasure in the picnic had dissipated, and she felt an ironic twist of disappointment as her gaze took in the pretty dishes, the romantic lighting, the mockingly cheerful checkered cloth.

"Still," she said softly, "you would wheedle any old memory out of me and use it against my father's wishes." It was a harsh thought.

His cheeks turned dark with color, and he ran a hand back through his hair. He looked as if he wanted to say she'd misunderstood him, but he stayed where he was, motionless, voiceless, as if he knew just how bad it looked. She needed no other proof of his intentions.

A cold weight dropped through her, leaving a ripple of bitterness. "I think I'll go home now," she said.

"No, Therese. Wait." He straightened and leaned nearer to her so that he was barely an arm's length away. "Your father never supported my efforts to find Beatrice's painting, but he respected my right to try. He warned me I would regret it if I ever brought Louisa back to Beatrice, but he was wrong." He shook his head, and the light gleamed on his dark hair. "The painting rightfully belongs to Beatrice and she deserves to have it."

"But my father didn't think so?" she asked. "Why not?"

Milo's gaze faltered for only an instant, then his eyes

met hers again, steady and truthful. "I don't know. That's the problem. He would never tell me."

His next unspoken question was obvious: Did she somehow know her father's secret?

Therese clenched her hand around the fragile stem of her wineglass, resisting the urge to get up and leave. "It doesn't make sense," she said. But what didn't make sense was that she still wanted to believe in him, even though he'd just proven he could plan a charming picnic simply in order to seduce a little information out of her. The idea hurt.

"Don't look at me like that," he said.

She closed her eyes but kept her chin level, hoping the turmoil in her heart would cease. "I've already told you," she said. "I don't know any of my father's secrets."

"You think that's the reason I brought you here?"

"Isn't it?"

When she heard his low chuckle, she opened her eyes, and relief washed through her. He was smiling easily, and as their gazes met, he reached forward to smooth a strand of hair back from her cheek.

"Your father's just an excuse," he said. "I wanted to hear you talk about yourself, and I thought memories of your dad would get you going."

"But there's a problem here," she said. "He didn't want Beatrice to have her picture back."

Milo nodded. "There's a problem here," he agreed. "Maybe we can figure it out together."

When he finished smoothing back the first strand, he found another, and the skin along her cheek and behind her ear was faintly electrified by his touch. She watched his eyes, waiting for him to look at her, but he kept his focus on her hair, and she felt him progress slowly down the length of her braid toward the blue ribbon at the end.

"Maybe you'll still tell me about yourself," he said. "Like, how old were you when you learned to braid your hair?"

She laughed. "Eleven. How old were you when you learned to tie your shoes?"

He lifted one eyebrow, his gaze on his fingers where they inspected her braid. "Boys are slower than girls with these things," he said.

"How old? Five? Six?"

"Seven," he said. "I was the best soccer player on my second-grade team, but my mom still had to tie my cleats for me."

"Do you still play?"

His eyes flicked up to hers, and he smiled when he saw that she was sincere. "I can tie my own cleats now, if that's what you're asking."

She laughed. The roots of her hair were beginning to lift on her scalp, even though his fingers were far away at the end of her braid. Then his hand trailed off to her arm and continued the gentle caress there, as if he were testing and teasing the silky fabric of her sleeve.

"My turn," she said.

He looked up, and she saw his eyes were nearly level with her own because of the way he leaned on his right arm.

"Your turn for what?" he asked.

Warmth slowly invaded her cheeks. "A question. We've already established that all the men I know have small apartments. But what about you? Do you always have to kidnap your dates?"

His eyes warmed as he smiled, and she noticed that faint lines appeared at the corners of his eyes when he was amused by something. He shifted slightly on the blanket, bringing himself nearer.

"The last woman I went out with told me I didn't have a soul."

Therese's eyebrows shot up.

He moved closer still. "The one before that told me I didn't have a heart."

She smiled. "And the one before that? There was one before that, I'm sure."

He came even nearer, until he was sitting just inches from her. "She told me I didn't have enough money."

She searched his eyes, trying to see how much he was joking and how much he spoke the truth. "Then what *did* they see in you?"

His gaze shifted unmistakably to her lips. She held her breath, caught between fear and an awful surge of longing. It couldn't be that his past relationships had been based purely on physical chemistry. She couldn't believe it. Yet he was the most sensually appealing man she'd ever seen. Even now, a sort of animal grace emanated from him, a wildness that threatened to scorch the tame flowers of the solarium and her own heart as well.

"I think," he said, tipping his face slightly and looking into her eyes, "I think, possibly, they saw reflections of themselves. And after a while they didn't like what they saw."

She felt her heart charge full of energy and beat rapidly behind her lungs. Glancing down, she saw she'd nervously twisted Milo's fortune into the tiniest shred of a coil. With a flash of inspiration, she lifted the paper, set it on the tip of her tongue, and swallowed it down.

Milo's eyes gleamed darkly as he watched her and a smile hovered over his sensual lips. "Finally," he said.

He'd known all along what she would do with it.

"You're the strangest person I've ever known," she said, her voice low and husky. She could almost taste his lips, he was so near. She saw him shift his weight slightly, then felt the caress of his fingers slide up her arm.

"And you have the most maddening integrity," he said.

He leaned near, then even nearer, his eyes as mesmerizing as a charm, until his lips met hers.

FOUR

Therese closed her eyes and let the pleasure of his warm kiss steal through her. Her chest tightened with a rush of emotion, and she leaned forward, barely aware that she was stepping into a chasm with no promise of a safe escape. Though the pull she felt toward his body was tantalizingly powerful, they were hardly touching, only meeting where their lips came together.

Still, she could feel the heat of him bridging the space between them, an invisible fire that pleaded to the need in her own chest. She forgot that Milo was probably an expert in seduction. She forgot that earlier she'd wanted to leave. She forgot everything but the silky heat that was spreading steadily through her body, awakening nerve endings she'd never known she had.

He slid his hand around her waist, and she leaned into him, molding her body against his strong torso so that the cotton of his shirt and the silk of her blouse fused into one thin, tantalizing barrier. He was as warm and solid as she'd remembered from their earlier kiss, but she sensed an added tension now, an unspoken expectation of intimacy that hinted at the latent power in his gentle hands. He pulled her even nearer, his kiss deepening, and she ran her hand up his shoulder and around to the warm nape of his neck. Of their own volition, her fingers threaded into his thick hair, memorizing the texture.

She felt no inner hesitation, only the awareness of Milo's hard body as he pressed against her. His hand ran around the silky fabric of her blouse, and she felt the warmth of his touch through the material as his fingers skimmed her midriff. When they found a way under her blouse to her sensitized skin, she felt a melting of anticipation; and when his knuckles grazed the lacy underside of her bra, she felt a slow-motion detonation explode in her mind.

He seemed to know instinctively the extent of her response, for he shifted his weight again to settle back against the carpet and cushions, retaining his intimate contact with her. Her nipples hardened as they pressed against the muscled strength of his chest, and the agonizing pleasure of it sent a ripple of abandon through her body. With her eyes closed, she kissed the inviting curve of his jaw, then the sensitive area of his neck that had always tempted her, half hidden by his collar. His warm skin smelled intoxicatingly masculine, strangely inviting, and it made her wonder how it would feel to press her cheek against his bare shoulder, his chest. Fingers fumbling at the unfamiliar task, she loosened the knot on his tie, then slipped it free. She worked her fingers around the top button of his shirt and eased it loose, then froze, waiting to see how he'd respond. When he burrowed his face in her hair, she dared to slide her fingers inside his shirt, to the heat of his chest, and she heard him utter a low groan.

She could feel his hand gliding down her skirt, her hip, and her mind went on hold, half hoping and half fearing that he'd reach underneath to her stocking. She bent her knee, and his warm palm slid around and behind her thigh, then he was smoothing his hand up her leg, and a rush of heat and longing spread through her body. She felt the exact moment when his fingers found the first inch of bare skin above her stocking, when he realized there was only skin and satin garter and a paradise of expectation between where his fingers lingered and her panties began.

He moaned and cuddled her more closely against his hips, rocking her there so she could make no mistake about the strength of his arousal.

She slowly lifted her heavy eyelids to find him gazing at her with such ferocity, such scrutinizing hunger, that her heart leaped with an instant of fear. But she saw something else besides his predatory need, a distant watchfulness that beckoned to her. His chest was rising and falling beneath hers with a raggedness that proved he was as affected as she was.

"Come upstairs with me," he said.

Her lungs ached with desire, but she stilled her hands, one still around his neck, the other nestled against the bare triangle of his chest. He wrapped his fingers tightly around hers, pressing her hand against his heart so that the beating there burned into her.

"Say you'll come with me," he urged quietly.

Slowly she shook her head and dropped her gaze

away. Her cheeks burned. Her lips were heavy and swollen from their kisses.

She longed to go with him, longed to finish this and finally ease the burning he'd ignited in her. But she was afraid too. She'd always believed she would know when she met the right man and that she'd have no question about committing herself totally, but never before had her body been ahead of her, begging her to go forward while her mind and heart were unsure. She couldn't reason it through clearly, wouldn't be able to explain it, but she felt the uncertainty in her heart.

She should never have let them get this far.

She felt his arms loosening around her and his fingers released her hand, leaving it feeling strangely cold and small. Glancing back at his face, she saw that his eyes had become more watchful. He wanted her still, she could see that, but he'd read her hesitation correctly. With his shirt unbuttoned in a deep V, his hair mussed and dark, he looked like a god of temptation and virility, and she was both tantalized and awed at the effect she had on him.

"Perhaps," he said, his tone deceptively reasonable, "since your answer isn't yes, you wouldn't mind moving off me."

Burning with embarrassment, she sat back, twisting her blouse around into a semblance of modesty. "I'm sorry," she said.

His eyes flashed. "Never apologize to me."

"I just don't want you to think I'm a tease."

He smiled strangely but otherwise remained motionless, still leaning back against the cushions. "You'd rather have me believe you could go ahead with this, even though you don't fully want to? You'd rather have me coerce you? I don't see myself as a man who has to confuse and seduce an innocent woman, thank you. Even a woman as tempting as you."

Her chin shot up, though inside Therese winced at his sarcasm. She didn't feel innocent, not when she was with Milo, yet she couldn't pretend she was experienced with recreational sex. That was what he wanted, wasn't it?

"I don't understand," she said finally. She gestured around the solarium, indicating the picnic, the calculated ambiance of the beautiful room.

Milo sat up. "Let's just say I was hopeful. There has been this unaccountable attraction between us ever since we met. Don't try to deny it. I thought maybe if we . . ." He frowned. "I thought it might clear the air if we made love. But it doesn't seem to have worked."

She said nothing. He stood, then reached a hand down to her. She tentatively put her hand in his and instantly felt the heat of his touch as he pulled her upright. They were standing near again, so near she would only have to tip her face upward slightly and his lips would be against hers.

"Unless," he said, his voice dangerously seductive, "you want to change your mind. We'd be good together, Therese. If you could put aside your reservations."

Her mind was still a riot of emotions. Even now she longed to close the distance between them, to simply melt against him and let him make love to her. It would be so easy; yet it was beyond impossible.

"I don't think it would clear the air between us," she said softly. "If that's your goal."

She watched his lips tighten into a thin line and she knew he was debating whether or not to kiss her again.

She was deathly afraid that if he did, she wouldn't be able to stop him a second time. He would be able to "confuse and seduce" her easily if he chose.

He slid his hands up her arms and turned her away from him.

"Remind me to support the Clean Air Fund," he said, his voice warm and resonant beside her ear.

Fighting her disappointment and frustration, she bit back confused tears. Then she felt his breath on her neck, and he brought her back against him, gently pushed her braid aside, and kissed the tender hollow below her right ear.

"I've never made love with anyone before," she said.

She could hear his chuckle against her hair.

"Just in case I hadn't figured that out?" he asked.

She smiled, cherishing the tenderness in his voice. "I just wouldn't want you to think it was you, personally, I object to."

"Ah. I see. That clears up everything. Air included."

She laughed quietly and leaned her head back against his shoulder. "Earlier tonight, when you were getting the Chinese food, I was wishing we could be friends."

He shook his head. "Sorry. Not possible."

"I know," she whispered.

He wrapped his arms around her, cradling her against him until she felt the power of his self-control, the patience that reined in his desire for her. The renewed rush of heat flushing her body told her unmistakably that it would fight to convince the rest of her that it was right, that she belonged in Milo's arms, receptive and willing. The unspoken truth was set like a time bomb between them, ticking expectantly, because it was no longer a question of if they would make love. It was only a matter of when.

He was unlike any person she'd ever known before. Suave, funny when she didn't expect it, smart, intense, attractive. Make that devastatingly attractive. And sexy. When Therese thought of the night in his solarium, her whole bone structure became liquid. Nobody had ever had this effect on her before, not even Josh, her fiancé. And with the few dates she'd had since then, it had been easy to keep her distance and never let anything get too physical. She'd even wondered if she was just naturally a solitary person, someone who didn't need physical passion the way other people did.

But not anymore.

She was ravenous too. In the small kitchen at work, she toasted a bagel, then spread it with cream cheese and peach jam. Then she ate another one and licked her fingers, while her assistant, Kate, watched her from the doorway with a curious smile.

"There's somebody on the phone for you," Kate said. "Shall I take a message?"

"Man or woman?" Therese asked.

Kate's eyebrows lifted a fraction higher. "Man. Very smooth voice. Sounds impatient and important. I'd guess a Gemini."

Therese felt the tingling begin in the backs of her knees and elbows. She was certain it was Milo. Her first instinct was to bolt for the phone, but she licked a last bit of jam from her index finger.

"Ask him if he'll hold," she said.

Kate gave her a quizzical look, then disappeared around the doorway.

Therese caught a glimpse of her reflection in the mirror over the counter and silently asked herself why she was stalling. Touching her cheek, she saw the parallel move of her reflection and felt the light coolness of her own fingers, like a faint trace of the kisses Milo had given her the previous night. He was waiting on the phone, she thought. But she couldn't go yet.

She was wearing a pearly gray blouse of raw silk, with touches of pale pink at the collar and an unusual line of antique buttons. She pivoted slightly before the mirror, testing the effect over her breasts and waist, almost as if she thought he'd be able to see her when she was on the phone.

You're going crazy, Therese.

In the mirror a pair of serious blue eyes looked back at her with the hooded concentration she knew from self-portraits. Her hair was a deep black that gleamed almost blue, held neatly by a bunchy ribbon at the nape of her neck. But then slowly she smiled, as if she were telling herself a secret. When she couldn't bear it anymore, she walked out to her phone, to where she could hit the hold button and see if he was still waiting.

"Therese here," she said softly. "Sorry to keep you waiting." With a quick glance at Kate, she turned her face to the partition, taking advantage of the privacy it offered.

"This is Milo. Do you always keep people waiting this long?"

She laughed, feeling a strange thrill. "Only you. What's up? Are you calling from the studio?"

"From home," he said. "How'd you sleep?"

"Fine. Why?"

"I hardly slept at all. I feel stiff all over. I've been kicking myself for letting you get away last night."

She smiled and coiled the phone cord around her wrist. "Thanks for the picnic," she said.

"That's all you can think about? The food?"

She liked the sound of his voice, half annoyed, half teasing. He almost sounded lonely.

"My grandmother always taught me to be polite after a first date," she said, "no matter if I had a good time or not. She said I could always say no a second time, but I had to be polite."

Milo growled something unintelligible.

"What?" Therese asked.

"Nothing. I'm calling because I have some news. Beatrice and her daughter are flying in today."

Therese felt her eyebrows lift in genuine surprise. "Were you expecting them?" she asked.

"No. At least not for several weeks."

Therese scratched the back of her head, then exhaled on a low whistle. Her eyes scanned, unseeing, a pile of papers on her desk as she tried to guess what it would mean for the painting and what it would mean for her and Milo.

"So will you be at the studio tonight?" she asked.

"That's the problem. You'll have to take a cab. Bert will stay with you."

She tried to stem the disappointment she felt. Bert was one of the security guards who remained with the portrait when Milo wasn't with it, and she had hardly paid attention to him before, besides saying hello when they met occasionally. His company would be nothing compared to Milo's. She felt her shoulders sag and was glad Milo couldn't see her after all.

"Therese?" he asked.

"I'm here."

"I'm sorry," he said. "She's old and the jet lag will make her cranky. I've got to settle her into a hotel and see that she has everything she needs. She wants me to look up a couple of her friends, locate a restaurant she half remembers, and get her some fresh baguettes."

Therese laughed. "Wouldn't she rather stay in your house?"

"Without round-the-clock maid service? I'm afraid not. And it's just as well. The cleaning service doesn't come until tonight, and the solarium still . . . Well, it still needs a bit of straightening up."

Therese could just imagine what the solarium looked like in the coolness of the afternoon, with the cushions still askew and the furniture pushed aside.

"I could have stayed to help you tidy up," she said.

"If you had stayed, there would have been a lot more to tidy up," he said dryly. "You might be here still."

She smiled as the idea of spending a night and a morning with Milo took hold in her mind. He'd be an amazing sight to wake up to, with his dark hair tumbling around his face, his eyes warm from sleep. She shifted slightly in her chair, startled and pleased at the new direction her mind was capable of taking.

"So what about tomorrow?" she asked. "I'll see you then?"

"Beatrice is having a couple of friends over and I'm expected."

She felt her heart sink. "Saturday?"

"A concert."

It was almost getting funny now. "Sunday?"

"We're driving down to see some of Beatrice's friends in Newport for the day."

"You mean Newport, Rhode Island? That pretty little town where all the mansions are?"

"Her friends have a summer cottage there. With ten bedrooms."

"An intimate little place," she said with understanding. She could just imagine him sitting at tea with Beatrice's wealthy, elderly friends, in the dining room of an enormous mansion. It hadn't taken long for him to be sucked back into his regular life: busy schedule, elite friends, sophisticated lifestyle. He'd once described it as formal and humorless, but clearly it had its rewards. And it didn't take a genius to see she didn't fit into it.

"Will you see the ocean?" she asked.

"Oh, Therese."

She bit her lip, aware she'd betrayed some of her loneliness. If only she could have half an hour with him to walk on a winter beach, to see the waves and to hold hands and hug each other. That's how she'd spend a day in Newport if she could. If he ever invited her along.

"Let's have dinner Monday night," he said.

She fiddled idly with the gadgets in her desk drawer and brought out a paper clip, which she began to bend. She wasn't sure how, but it changed things having Beatrice and her daughter in town. "We've already had takeout," she said. "Remember? You were planning to clear the air between us."

"This will be at a real restaurant. Just us. Regular air. I promise."

She pushed out her lips, considering. "Give me one good reason why I should go with you."

"You like to eat."

She smiled. "This is true."

"You can have all the cheesecake with chocolate-cookie crust you can eat."

She was strangely touched that he remembered. "Good memory."

"You don't have to pay for your half of the check," he added.

"Oh. Now that's good."

His low chuckle came over the phone, and she smiled again.

"I'll pick you up from the museum at six."

"What is this masterful tone?" she objected. "Is that supposed to be cool or something? Do you practice it? Is it like your macho driving?"

She could hear him groan.

"Would you just say yes for once?"

"No," she said, smiling.

But she was pretty sure he got the idea.

Therese spent the next few evenings working in the studio with Bert sitting in the chair by the desk. This was the first time one of the two security guards had been there with her. Always before, Milo had stayed with her and she saw the guard—usually Bert—only as she and Milo were leaving for the night and the guard was arriving. Bert was a quiet, round-faced man in his early forties who liked to knit. His wife was expecting their first baby, he told Therese, and he was working on a little white sweater. Therese found it curious to see such a muscular, reserved man with white yarn laced around his thick fingers, but she had no doubt he took his work as a security guard seriously. He was alert to every sound and had installed window blinds on six of the eight windows. The last two needed different hardware, and Therese knew Bert had mentioned this as a priority to Milo. Personally, she liked having the blinds up, even at night. She liked seeing the windows of the building opposite, to remind her of other people working and living, so the studio wasn't so lonely.

It was awful being there without Milo. She tried to concentrate on Louisa, and she did manage to keep her work moving along steadily, but she missed Milo's presence, his offers of coffee, the small noises of concentration he made when he worked at his computer. She hoped Beatrice would go back to Paris soon, so she and Milo could resume their companionable nights in the studio.

When Therese arrived at the studio on the third night, Sunday night, Bert had his coat on and was standing with the portable phone to his ear.

"Thank goodness you're here," he said, setting the phone in its cradle. "My wife's having labor pains. I've been trying to reach Milo, but all I get is his answering machine. I can't reach the other security guard either. I've got to go. Whatever you do, don't leave the painting, okay?"

She laughed. "The painting is the last thing you have to worry about right now. Go already!"

Bert flashed her a quick, distracted grin and charged out the door. She could hear him running down the stairs and only hoped he didn't break his neck before he got to the hospital.

His excitement left her smiling long after he'd gone. A new baby was big news, she thought. She sat at her table, trying to work, but she was undeniably fidgety. It was the first time she'd been alone in the studio after dark, and Bert's protectiveness of the painting made her hope that nobody seriously wanted to steal it.

When the phone rang, she jumped. "Milo?" she asked, holding the receiver to her ear.

There was silence, then a soft click.

"Hello?" she said.

But the line was dead.

Uneasy, she looked up Milo's number and gave him another call, but he still didn't answer. Was he at a concert or in Newport? she wondered, trying to remember.

"Please call me when you get in," she said after the beep. "It's important."

She hoped she wasn't exaggerating.

She paced once around the studio, checking to make sure the door was locked and looking out the windows for anything unusual. Releasing the taut nylon cords one after another, she let down the blinds that covered the six windows closest to the bed.

It was nothing, she told herself. Big-city girl. No reason to get antsy.

Standing at one of the uncovered windows, she scanned the street below and the building opposite her. Now that it was March, the leaves had started budding and the tree branches reached to the windows, but the view to the building on the other side of the street was still pretty clear. Many of the windows were lit, pale yellow squares that Therese found reassuring. Then, in one window with no curtain, she saw a telescope set up, aimed at one of the windows higher up in her own building. The telescope was deserted, the peeping Tom out of sight, but it made her uncomfortable to know that a self-proclaimed voyeur was set up across the street from her.

She looked at Milo's bed and seriously considered taking the bedclothes and nailing them up over the last two windows.

Then she laughed at herself. *Now you're overreacting,* she thought. *Just get busy and forget it.*

She sat down before Louisa and forced herself to concentrate. In moments she was engrossed, and when she next thought to check out the window again, the light in the telescope apartment was off. Good, she thought.

Two hours later, just when Therese was thinking she'd want to go home soon, a knock sounded. Her heart expanded with relief. Maybe Milo forgot his key, she thought, standing stiffly. And then she considered that it could be Bert coming back. She couldn't wait to see the look on the new dad's face.

She automatically peeked through the peephole and her fingers froze on the deadbolt. A strange man was outside the door, a tall man with short blond hair who was wearing a suit. Her heart began to beat hard.

"Who is it?" she called.

"The name's Tony Miller. Bert Winston and I work together sometimes, and he asked me to fill in for him tonight since the other security guard is out of town. His wife just had their baby. It's a girl."

"That's great," Therese said, still hesitating. Bert hadn't mentioned a Tony to her, although he had said he'd tried in vain to reach the other security guard. Still . . . "This may sound a little paranoid, but do you have some identification or something?"

"Sure," he said, reaching into his pocket. Relieved, she watched through the peephole as he pulled out a wallet. He disappeared from sight and a driver's license slid under the door.

She picked it up, checking the photo. It was Tony Miller all right. Then the phone rang.

"Just a second," she said.

She picked up the portable phone and reached back for the door, unlocking the deadbolt.

"Hello?" she said into the phone.

"It's a boy!" Bert's voice boomed.

Not a girl. Raw horror coursed through her, paralyzing her, then she flipped the bolt closed again, locking out the man in the hall.

FIVE

Therese gripped the phone with all her might.

"Bert?" she whispered.

"It's a boy!" he yelled. "Can you stand it? And Nancy's just fine! She's incredible! You never saw anything like it!"

"Bert!" she said fiercely, watching the door in terror. Any second the man on the other side would realize what had happened.

"Get Milo here *now*," she said. "There's a man named Tony Miller outside the door and he said he was a security guard you sent."

Bert swore. "I didn't send anybody. Get down. And turn out the lights. You'll be okay. These people aren't out to hurt anybody. He just wants the painting."

"Hello?" The man outside jiggled the doorknob. "You in there?"

"Oh, please, Bert!" She dropped to the floor and crawled away from the door.

"You going to let me in?" the man asked.

She was still gripping the phone. "Coming!" she called in what she hoped was a normal voice. "Bert," she whispered. "What do I do?"

"Stall him. I'll be there in five minutes," Bert said, and hung up.

Was he crazy? Therese thought.

She crawled backward until she was in the far corner of the studio, the kitchenette, and stood for an instant to flick off the lights. Listening anxiously, she waited, her eyes adjusting to the dark and her knees pressed against the wooden floor. A plane passed overhead. She could hear her own ears click as she swallowed thickly. But nothing more.

Was he still out there? She hadn't heard him move away.

She was still clutching the phone, and now she jabbed at the buttons, dialing 911.

"You've got to help me," she whispered as the dispatcher answered.

Suddenly there was a sharp bang at the door, as if the man had kicked it. Therese screamed. The door held tight.

"There's a man trying to break in!" she yelled into the phone. "You've got to send somebody quick!"

"We'll send a car right away," said the dispatcher. "Stay calm. I just need to confirm your address."

"Calm?" she gasped, then choked out her location. She looked frantically around the room, then remembered the fire escape. She ran across the room and tried to open the window, but she had to use both hands, so she dropped the phone.

Any second she expected the door to be bashed open.

She wrenched the window upward and a sharp breeze came into the studio. She groped for the phone and took it with her, getting one leg and then the other out onto the steel fire-escape landing. She peeked back in the studio, but the door was still closed and she heard no second bang.

"Are you still with me?" the police dispatcher asked.

"I'm out on the fire escape!" She glanced down wildly at the ground two floors below. "Oh, please! Send somebody fast!"

She heard the sound of the siren before the dispatcher could say anything more, and Therese was so relieved, she nearly fell off the fire escape. She could see the lights of the police car reflecting off the buildings as it approached. Thank God, she thought, and told the dispatcher they had come. She waited until the police announced themselves at the door with a teeth-rattling knock, then jumped back through the window and raced across the studio to open the door.

She'd never been so happy to see anybody.

"Hi," she said, her voice sounding strangled.

"You all right? Is the intruder gone?" one of the officers asked.

She nodded, then flipped on the light. She was shaking all over, but the raw panic had left her heart. "A man came and said he was filling in for the security guard who's usually here. He left his ID."

The officers entered the studio, and one of them picked up the driver's license and put it in a bag.

Therese's shaking got worse. She had to sit down. She stepped over to the bed and sat on the edge, gripping her hands together to try to stop them from trembling.

At the sound of footsteps pounding up the stairs, both officers sprang into defensive positions, then Milo ran into the room. He looked furious and horror-struck, like he was ready to murder somebody himself. When he saw the police, he slowed to a halt and showed his empty hands, but he still looked furious. The police lowered their weapons, and with one rapid movement Milo took Therese into his arms.

"Are you all right?" he demanded.

She nodded, then closed her eyes. All she wanted to do was make the whole episode vanish from her mind.

Milo held her tight in his powerful arms. "What happened?" he asked. "I just talked to Bert. How long have you been here alone?"

She pulled back, and Milo loosened his arms.

One of the officers took out a pad of paper and began to ask her questions. She gave Milo's arm a squeeze, then sat down again on the bed. It took her only a few minutes to tell her story and explain the open window above the fire escape. The door had a dirt mark from the stranger's shoe, but otherwise there was no damage.

She could hardly believe it had happened. She pressed a hand against her throat, where her pulse still ran rapidly. She didn't dare look at Milo because she knew the repressed anger in his face would frighten her all over again.

"If you see him again," one officer said to her, "be sure to call. We'll check out the apartment with the telescope across the street. You might consider staying somewhere else for a few days if you're nervous. If he was after the painting, as Mr. Dansforth here suggests, you should move that as well. We can see if this Tony Miller has a record and begin an investigation. I'll have the patrol keep an eye on the building, but use your own caution as well."

Therese nodded grimly. She felt violated, even though the man hadn't made it inside the studio. What if the police hadn't responded so quickly? What if she'd had to start down that fire escape in the dark? What if she'd opened the door in the first place, as she'd been about to do?

The officer shook his head sympathetically, as if he could read her fear. "I'm sorry this happened, Ms. Carroll. We'll do our best to look out for you."

Therese stood and reached out to shake hands. "Thanks for coming so fast," she said.

They tested the lock on the door on their way out, then closed the door, leaving Milo and Therese alone in the studio.

The wind still rushed in through the window over the fire escape and Milo crossed quickly to shut it. With the soft thump of the window, the quiet of the room expanded toward the corners, but it wasn't the comfortable silence she'd known before. She closed her eyes, trying to erase the last vestiges of her fear. She trembled once, reflexively, then took a long, steadying breath.

"That was close," she whispered.

"Where is Bert?" Milo asked. His voice was steady, but there was a murderous look in his eyes.

"He was at the hospital with his wife. She just had a baby. Didn't you say you talked to him?"

"I cut him off. He was supposed to remain *here*."

Therese was surprised, then angry. "Well, where were *you?*" she asked. "Bert and I tried to reach you all night. You knew his wife was pregnant. You couldn't really expect him to stay away from her, could you?"

"I didn't know his wife was having her baby *tonight.*"

"Babies aren't exactly something you can schedule!" Therese spat back.

He put his hands on his hips and glared at her.

Of all the obstinate, unreasonable people, he had to be the worst, she thought. Now he actually blamed Bert for being a good husband.

"You're the one who cares so much about this stupid picture," she said, giving full vent to her anger. "You should have been here to guard it tonight, not me."

"I was coming here anyway when he finally reached me."

She raged on regardless. "I might have broken my neck trying to get down that fire escape and then what would have happened to the painting?"

Milo stalked back toward her. "If I'd been here ten minutes sooner, none of this would have happened."

"I hate heights! And what if I'd let him in? I almost let him in!"

"Bert had orders not to leave you alone here."

"Would you quit blaming Bert!" she snapped. "It's just a dumb painting!"

Milo's eyes burned into hers. "Bert should have told you to leave when he did. It's not the painting I care about," he said fiercely. "It's you."

Her heart did a quick gold-medal dive. "What?" she whispered.

He came nearer. And he was still angry. "You heard

me. I never meant to put you in danger. You should have left the painting unguarded rather than put yourself in jeopardy."

She felt her jaw drop half an inch, then she mechanically closed it back up. She, Therese Carroll, was more important to him than his painting of Louisa de Plentagon, the work of his life? Did he know what he was saying?

From where he stood beside the desk, she could see the smoldering anger, the residual fear that tightened the muscles in his face and jaw. His eyes were sharp and dark under his black eyebrows, and she faltered before his ferociousness.

Therese looked down at the carpet beneath her shoes while her heart beat erratically in her chest. Too much was happening to her. She could feel the trembling starting again in her fingers and arms.

She looked up when the lights went off. Milo had moved quietly over to the switch and stood there now, waiting, while the room was flooded with soft spring darkness and dim reflections from the streetlights below.

"Are you still scared?" he asked.

A little, she thought. But she didn't answer.

"Thomas is a fool," Milo went on. "I have no doubt in the world that he was behind this. And I'll put an end to it when I call him tomorrow. You don't need to be worried, Therese. You're safe now. I promise."

With a final, ragged shiver, she felt the last of her horror ease away. Whoever Thomas was, Milo could take care of him. "I know," she whispered. She was safe because she was with him.

All the windows had their blinds down except the last

two, and as her eyes slowly undilated, she could make out the motionless, shadowed form of Milo as he waited, still waited, by the light switch. The tension between them thickened, seeming to slow time. The shadowy dimness reminded her of a very old painting, one with varnish that had darkened so much that only the most dramatic lines were still visible. Milo was one of those lines.

"We don't want any telescopes on us," he said quietly, providing a belated explanation for why he'd turned off the lights.

Her adrenaline kicked into overdrive. She watched him walk toward her, the reflected light dancing subtly over his body. He dropped his leather coat on a chair and came a couple of steps nearer.

She swallowed hard.

"I've been wanting you nonstop for three days," he said quietly. "And now I know why."

She felt her chest expand with fear and a crazy hope. "Why's that?" she asked.

"Don't you know?"

She shook her head. He came closer, his shoes noise- less on the carpet, so he was hardly more than a shadow. Until he touched her. When his warm, strong fingers brushed against her cheek, she felt a surge of liquid heat through her body and instinctively leaned toward him. He held himself away, yet tantalizingly near.

"Tell me honestly," he said. "Try to tell me you don't feel what's between us."

"I don't—"

But before she could voice her doubts, his lips stole the breath from her mouth and she was crushed in his embrace. She felt the ache inside her spread out and claim her with an awful, delicious yearning. Wrapping her arms around his neck, she pulled herself nearer, stretching up on tiptoe to imprint the intensity of her feeling with her kiss. Her lips parted willingly and the edge of his tongue rasped against them, driving a stinging heat through her core.

"Your body doesn't lie, Therese," he said. His eyes bored into hers, demanding her to acknowledge the truth. "We need to be together tonight."

She settled back down on her heels, but his strong arms refused to let her slip free. It amazed her how easily he read her, how he welcomed her instinctive advances and resisted when she sought to withdraw. She tried to sort through her mixed feelings. It wasn't that she wasn't attracted to him. Heaven knew she was. And it wasn't that she believed any longer that he didn't really care for her; she knew the night's events had had a powerful effect on him. It was her own heart she distrusted. Years of relying on herself had trained her to protect herself when she felt vulnerable, and she definitely felt vulnerable now.

"My body has to live with the rest of me tomorrow," she said, trying to make her voice sound light.

He frowned down at her. "And you think you'd regret spending the night with me? Why?"

"I'm not sure." It was as honest as she could be.

"Are you afraid I'd hurt you?"

She shook her head slowly. "Not physically. No."

Physically, she was intensely curious, and he had to know that. But emotionally she didn't know if she was ready to risk being intimate with him. That was the problem.

"But I could only hurt you in another way if it mattered to you," he said. "If it mattered a lot to you."

She nodded.

He pulled her nearer and nestled her head against his shoulder. She closed her eyes tightly, feeling her heart swell at the tender strength of his touch.

"That's why, Therese. That's why this is right. It matters to me too."

He used one finger to tip her chin up and his eyes searched hers. His heavy lids hooded his expression, but she could read the quiet depths beneath his passion, like a dark stone beneath the surface of a rippling stream. He lingered a moment longer, giving her a last opportunity to consider, then his lips descended again, and she knew this time there was no going back.

As the last taut string of hesitancy snapped, she felt a rush of desire and certainty, a conviction that she was making the right choice even if she didn't yet know the reasons. All the passion she'd kept locked deep inside her came flooding out, and she kissed him with a kind of amazed despair. She wanted him so badly it hurt her inside, and she wanted him to go quickly.

But Milo had other ideas. His lips moved to her temple, then down her jaw, seeking and finding the sensitive hollow beneath her ear. She felt the cool silver of her earring being brushed out of his way along her neck, then his lips moved lower, to the aching pulse of her throat.

Therese moaned and slid her hands up his back, feeling the hard muscles beneath the fine fabric of his shirt. There was no way to fight his pace. She'd have to slow down with him and luxuriate in every subtle move, whether she wanted to or not. He smelled faintly of mint and some other dry, warm scent, as if his leather coat had rubbed its distinctive smell into his cotton shirt. She fingered the line of his collar, then slipped her fingers in against the warm skin of his throat. On tiptoe, she set her next kiss on the invisible trail left by her fingers and had the infinite pleasure of knowing this time she'd get to explore further.

Milo's hands spanned her back, and with one hand poised there to steady her, he used the other hand to explore the sensitive area where her hip met her waist. She was wearing black jeans and a simple black silk chemise with a deep blue cashmere cardigan over it, and when his fingers slipped beneath the sweater, she instantly felt the silk absorb his heat and burn lightly around her waist as he caressed her there.

"You've never worn jeans before," he murmured.

"It's the weekend," she answered, her voice low and raspy.

His lips claimed hers again, and a spiral of need began to build in her gut. Her breasts felt swollen and tight beneath the chemise, and her sweater was growing uncomfortably hot. She reached behind her neck to pull off the sweater, but his hands skimmed quickly up her arms and with deft, sure movements he helped her take it off.

Her braid fell back down and swished once across her breasts. She could see the way his gaze followed the movement, could feel how her own ragged breathing highlighted the outline of her breasts under the delicate chemise. In the dim light his face was shadowed and lined, but his eyes watched her possessively, with unspoken hunger. She could feel his hands at her waist, his thumbs kneading gently at the edge of her waistband, then he stroked upward with both hands, stopping only when he reached the undersides of her breasts, where they swelled the lacy confines of her bra.

She inhaled sharply, tipping her chin up and arching her back slightly to invite his intimate touch. His thumbs just barely skimmed the taut peaks of her aching breasts, teasing through the silk and lace, and she felt a new surge of impatience.

Sliding nearer, inside his arms, she brushed her body against his, pivoting until she could feel his arousal straining and hard inside his pants. Then she lowered her hands and touched him shyly above his belt buckle. She gave his shirt an infinitesimal tug, and he sucked in his stomach, letting the shirt trail out of his slacks as she pulled it up.

He kissed her ear and murmured against her hair, "You're making it hard for me to stand."

She kissed him back and felt her own desire undoing the strength of her knees.

With a low growl, Milo swept his arm behind her knees and lifted her smoothly, his strength making her feel oddly weightless as he carried her the short distance to the bed. He laid her down and sat beside her, staring at her hungrily, then he pulled his shirt off, exposing a lean, muscled torso that made her fingers tingle with the need to touch him.

"You can't imagine how many nights when you were working I wanted to bring you right here," he said. He leaned over her and kissed her lightly. "And you wouldn't even stop for coffee with me."

He ran his palm along her flat stomach, spreading the growing heat through her so that she reached for him, wanting him nearer. But he held himself up with one arm and used the other hand to stroke her so persistently, so relentlessly, that she felt both tense and relaxed, hot and feather light. When he finally pushed her chemise off to cup his palm under her breast, a groan escaped her and she pulled against his neck with both hands, urging him nearer. But instead of kissing her lips, his mouth found the sensitive peak of her breast and sucked through the thin material of her bra, sending an agony of desire through her.

Therese wanted to touch all of him, wanted to skim her hands down the planes of his back to the firm contours of his hips and lower. She had watched him so many times, when he was turning to put away a coat or leaning against a counter, that she felt she already had a mental map for how his body was laid out. But she wanted to travel the journey with her own hands and feel the fine texture of his heated skin. She tugged at the buckle of his pants, but it resisted her fingers, while he seemed to have no trouble at all undoing the snap and zipper of her jeans. She could feel them being eased down her hips, so the cool air touched her lower abdomen and panties, and once one knee was free, she easily kicked the jeans off the rest of the way.

Finally Milo's fingers closed over hers and he undid his belt. He stood up long enough to loosen his pants, then shucked them and his briefs to the floor. For one long moment he paused there in the shadowy light, watching her, and she let her gaze travel from his eyes, past his lips, down the hard contours of his chest to his stomach, then lower, to his magnificent arousal. He seemed proud and completely unself-conscious under her gaze, and she longed to know how he'd respond if she touched him.

He slid beside her on the bed, and she tentatively stroked her hand down his abdomen, pausing in the tangles below, and looked into his face to be certain.

Inches from her own, his eyes pleaded with her, and he touched her ever so gently on her arm, as if to encourage her forward. She closed her fingers around him and heard him sigh in consummate pleasure. She tried easing her thumb around him, and he seemed to freeze for a long moment. Then he pulled her roughly against him and began a new assault on her senses.

She realized why he'd been pacing himself before, because his teasing tenderness now gave way to more insistent desire. His hands found the front clasp of her bra and released it so that her swelling breasts, once released, were only momentarily relieved before they pulsed with an even deeper ache. When he pressed his full length on top of her, she welcomed his weight, as if she had to feel his hot skin against her own or lose her sanity.

And then she felt his fingers at the edge of her panties, stroking there, teasing, until she rolled her hips in unconscious invitation. He ground his hips against hers as if to slow her, but a sensual dance had started in her nerves, a liquid rhythm that could no longer be denied. She desired him with an abandon that frightened and claimed her, changing something inside her permanently as she accepted this new truth into her heart. In one instant she was both supremely powerful and utterly helpless, and she knew that once he'd possessed her, she would never be the same again.

In a moment her panties were gone and there was

nothing between them. She shuddered as his fingers found her intimate folds, and she whispered his name, urging him to hurry. He kissed her, telling her to hold on for one more moment, then he reached into the drawer of the bedside stand for protection. In the space of a breath he was poised above her again, and she could see his strong shoulders bridging her, his eyes watching her with a hungry longing that seared into her soul. She touched him again with both her hands, feeling the heat and power in his need. She didn't believe she could wait any longer.

He entered her, nudging in so gradually that she had no thought for pain, only the driving urgency of her own desire. She lifted her hips to meet him, craving the closeness that she instinctively knew would satisfy the shimmering ache inside her. Still he held back, still he controlled his progress, while she beckoned him forward. She tried to think of some way to bring him nearer and finally circled her knees up while she used all her strength to pull herself upward, pressing her breasts against his chest. He was unable to hold on any longer, and he drove deeply into her, thrusting with such force that she gasped in sudden pain.

Milo froze inside her. She held her hands on his waist, keeping him still, trying to give her body a chance to absorb the tingling shock that was rippling through her. He waited, watching her with infinite care, while the skin of his forehead gleamed faintly with the strain of his effort and his dark eyes searched her soul. And then slowly an exquisite sensation began building in her, half burning, half cool, and she found herself rocking slightly with a new, inner rhythm. She saw Milo close his eyes again, then lean his head down to kiss her lips. The rhythm spread through her, erasing the last of her pain, becoming stronger and stronger until she was intensely, physically alive. She cried out with the savage pleasure of it, and Milo drove into her again, this time sending a honeyed sweetness through her, a promise her body knew would be fulfilled. And when the charges began to go off, one after another, Therese gasped at the incredible beauty of it and urged him on with the eager rhythm of her body. Just as she thought it could get no more spectacular, she felt a final release of pleasure, and knew that Milo, too, was shattering inside.

Several hours later Therese slipped quietly out of the bed and tucked the covers around Milo's shoulders. She backed one step away and he opened his eyes so quickly, she thought he must have been awake.

"Where are you going?" he asked.

"I'll be right back," she said.

"You're not leaving."

"No," she whispered. She went into the bathroom, where she washed up and slipped into the white towel she found on the back of the door. When she came back out, Milo was sitting up in the bed with a small light on.

"Couldn't you sleep?" he asked.

She shook her head. "I'm too wired. Is it bad etiquette to get out of bed after . . . ? You know."

He smiled and reached out a hand. She let the towel drop and sat next to him, snuggling her knees under the blanket. Shifting an arm around her back, he settled her comfortably next to him so that their heads were braced against the pillows and the teak headboard.

"What's keeping you up?" he asked.

"Everything. Tonight. The break-in. Being with you. So much has happened."

He kissed her shoulder and took her hand in his. Stroking her fingers, he asked, "Are you okay?" His voice was very low, very intimate.

She nodded.

"I didn't want to hurt you," he said gravely. "I'm sorry, Therese."

"It only lasted a minute. And then it was fine. More than fine."

He lifted her fingers to kiss them. "For me too."

It seemed like he had more to add, but she squeezed his hand. She was afraid that if he kept talking in his deep, seductive voice, she'd hear something she didn't want to hear, some pretty lie she shouldn't believe. She couldn't believe tonight had meant as much to him as it had to her, and she couldn't bear to hear him try to tell her how special it had been. They'd made love. Something inside her had been ripped in two and forged back together more incredible than before. Her body had carried her far, far beyond where her reason told her she belonged. She would accept it all in the morning. But not tonight.

She couldn't bear to think that, for Milo, this amazing experience was something he had shared with any number of women.

"More than fine," she said again, her voice small. At least that much was true.

He turned his head to look at her, and she sensed his

gaze but refused to meet his eyes. Her cheeks burned under his scrutiny.

"What's this, Therese?" he asked.

She shook her head, but he wasn't put off.

"It was more powerful than either one of us could have predicted," he said. "I'm not quite sure what to make of it either, but I plan to figure it out." He traced the curve of her face, stopping at her chin. "You aren't going to pretend we're back to square one, are you?"

She heard the gentle humor in his voice, but didn't trust herself to respond.

If only he would tell her he loved her, if only she could believe him, it might begin to make some sense, she thought. But did that mean she was falling in love? Her heart gave a jolt, but her mind responded to the concept with a sort of fascinated horror. She turned to look at him, her eyes wide with uncertainty.

He instantly drew nearer and kissed her. "Don't look at me like that, Therese." He smoothed the loose tendrils of hair from around her face, and she closed her eyes at the cool touch of his palm on her cheek.

"Come here," he murmured, as if she weren't already only inches away. "We have tomorrow to work it out. And the next day. And the next."

He settled her more comfortably into his arms and pulled the soft comforter up around her shoulders. She could feel him inhale deeply and knew he could feel her breathing too, with the arm he kept loosely around her.

"Let me tell you a story," he said.

"A bedtime story?"

She could feel his warm chuckle against her hair.

"Yes," he said. "Something from long ago and far away."

"Does it have dragons in it?"

"Not that long ago."

She laughed, letting her body relax against his. Closing her eyes, she readied her mind to imagine whatever he described. He slowly stroked her hair, his touch feather light.

"There once was a young man," he began, "a cynical type. He'd lost his parents, he'd spent time in jail, and in his own dark way he didn't care if he self-destructed. Well, this kid had an old soccer coach who cornered him one day and ordered him to get his act together. He lined up a job for the kid with his cousin in Paris. The kid didn't want to go, but the old coach ordered him to, so in the end he did."

Therese knew immediately that this story was something from Milo's own past, and wondered why he would talk about it as if it had happened to someone else.

"How did he do in Paris?" she asked.

Milo inhaled slowly. "At first he didn't like it. His job was painting houses and it was tedious and hot. It gave him too much time to think. But the man he worked for was a great guy: Orrin. He was a sculptor, with a wife and a couple of daughters. They were very open, spontaneous people, and they acted like the young man's moods were just a joke. They teased him, mainly, and gave him more work to do. The little girls bossed him around constantly."

Therese laughed. "I'll bet he didn't know what to make of them."

Milo trailed his fingers down her arm, lightly touching the skin on the inside crook of her elbow. "Yeah, at first. They were pretty cool, though."

She heard the faint echo in his voice, and she could imagine how he had been won over by this family's teasing friendship. He must have cared deeply for them.

"Is there more?" she asked.

He nodded. "One day Orrin and the cynical kid were painting an old farmhouse and the older daughter was with them. She was really wild; what you'd call high-spirited. She wanted to play soccer with the kid that day, but he told her he was too busy painting. So she got another ladder and climbed up to help."

"How old was she?" Therese asked.

"I don't know. Nine or ten."

Milo fell silent. His hand slowed on her arm and finally stopped.

She turned to try to see his face, but he was peering across the dim room as if he could look back in time.

"What happened?" she asked softly.

"The girl fell. The whole ladder just tipped slowly back while she held on near the top, and then it crashed onto the ground. She never even screamed."

Therese felt her stomach tighten with dread. "Oh, no. Was she all right?"

Milo slowly shook his head. "I had to drive them to the hospital," he said. "I had to drive them for forty-five minutes, and the whole time Orrin was sitting in the back, trying to hold her steady, praying to God that she'd keep breathing."

Therese heard the ache in his voice and waited silently for him to go on. It must have been a harrowing ride for all of them.

Finally he gave her a twisted smile. "She was okay in the end. She had a concussion and a broken arm, but she was up again and as wild as ever in another month."

Relief washed through her, and she smiled at Milo.

"And the cynical kid?" she asked. "Was he all right?"

Milo grumbled out a laugh, as if he realized he'd finally merged his story with true memory. "I thought Orrin would blame me, but he never did."

Therese gazed at his face, memorizing the line of his jaw in the soft light, loving the intimate rumble of his voice. She knew he was trying to tell her something else, something important. "Why are you telling me this?" she asked.

He tilted his face sideways, watching her closely. "I'll never forget driving them to the hospital," he said. "I could see them in the rearview mirror—that's what I still see—and something about the way Orrin held his daughter disturbed me so much, I almost couldn't drive. It's hard to explain."

Therese thought she understood. "He loved her so much. He was so worried about her."

"Yes," Milo said. He licked his lips and went on. "I think that was the first time I really, really understood that my parents were dead."

Therese didn't trust herself to speak. It was as if he'd told her he didn't believe anyone would ever love him again. She turned her body fully against him and put her arms around him, holding him near so that her cheek was pressed against his hair. Her heart ached for all he had lost.

"You're sweet to listen," he said finally.

She kissed his hair. "It must have been a hard time for you."

He shifted, and she loosened her arms so that he could tip his face toward her again. His eyes were warm and serious.

"It makes more sense to me now," he said. "I think, before that day, I didn't care what happened to me because no one else did either. But when I saw Orrin and his daughter, I knew my parents had loved me that much too. I knew that it would have broken their hearts to see what I'd become. It was as if a button clicked." He paused, seeming to search for the right words. "I had to take responsibility for my life, not to please my parents, really, but for myself. I had to be my own dad, in a way. Even if nobody else cared. No more excuses or crutches."

She thought she understood better how he'd been able to transform himself from a troubled kid into a successful art dealer. And yet she wondered if he'd lost something that day too. His poignant story touched her and reminded her of her own lost parents.

She smoothed a finger along his frowning eyebrows and tried a smile. "That's a lot from one look in the rearview mirror," she said.

He caught her fingers and pulled them against his lips for a kiss. His smile was warm with charm. "Are you saying you don't believe me?"

But she did. His story felt absolutely true to her. "I might believe you," she said.

" 'Might'?"

She rubbed her knuckles along his collarbone and into the dip at the base of his throat. "Have you ever told your mirror story to anyone else?"

His eyes locked with hers, his gaze steady. He was offering her a glimpse straight into the depths of his soul. "No," he said.

"I didn't think so," she said softly.

She knew instinctively that the emotional intimacy he shared with her was as precious, in its own way, as what they'd shared with their bodies. She knew, as he guided her head back to his shoulder and settled her easily against him so that they could relax into sleep, that the intricate ties of this night would never leave her.

SIX

"A long time ago, back between the wars, when Beatrice was a young girl, she lived with her family in the south of France, near the Pyrenees," Milo said. "Her grandmother on the de Plentagon side, Madame Sophie, was a real matriarch and she liked having her family around her. All the cousins in Beatrice's generation spent every summer in Madame Sophie's chateau, swimming and hiking and playing practical jokes."

"Sounds like a lot of fun," Therese said.

They were walking in the park across from the museum where Therese worked, enjoying the cool sunlight of her lunch hour. Therese loved walking beside him, matching her pace to his long-legged stride, knowing all she had to do was turn her head and she'd see the engaging planes of his face. She smiled and thought: *I made love with this man a mere twelve hours ago.* How was that for a shocker?

"Madame Sophie's favorite grandchild was Beatrice's cousin," Milo continued, "a boy named Thomas, who played the wildest jokes of all. When Madame Sophie died in 1949, she left all her wealth and property to Thomas, who was newly married; everything except certain tokens for each of the other grandchildren. The cousins began to argue. They felt the will was unfair. Beatrice was especially hurt because she had adored her grandmother, and all Madame Sophie had left to her, it seemed, was a single gaudy pearl."

Therese picked up on the key phrase. " 'It seemed'?" she echoed.

Milo reached down and picked up a stone, then sent it skimming over the little pond beside the path.

"Now remember," he said. "Madame Sophie was the granddaughter of the child bride, Louisa, our friend in the picture. Madame Sophie's will read like this: 'To my darling Beatrice, I direct Louisa's portrait and the jewelry in the picture.' That's all. No other specific description. And the worst of it was, the portrait of Louisa had been missing for years, ever since the First World War."

Therese frowned, puzzling it over. "How do you know all this?" she asked. She paused when they came to a little bridge, turning to lean back against the railing. Milo stopped beside her, bracing his hands on the railing.

"Beatrice told me," he said. "And I've seen a facsimile of Madame Sophie's will."

"But it doesn't make much sense. Why would Madame Sophie put a portrait in her will when she didn't even have the portrait anymore?"

She could see Milo contemplating the flow of the little stream below. The story was more involved than she'd expected, but she liked the glimpse into another time, another family.

"Apparently, Thomas once took the portrait for a practical joke," Milo explained. He idly roughed the hair back over his ears. "When it disappeared during the war, Madame Sophie must have believed Thomas had taken it again. Some of the cousins remembered her teasing Thomas about it, as if she appreciated a joke but expected he could produce the painting again on demand, if need be."

Therese laughed. "That's a little crazy."

He turned his head to smile at her, and she was momentarily distracted by how the sunlight fell on his dark hair and broad shoulders. "Crazier things happen in wills all the time."

She could believe that. "So what did they do?" she asked. "How did Beatrice end up with one pearl?"

"The cousins had to go by their memory of the old painting, from when it hung on a wall in the chateau. Everyone remembered the pearl necklace. A couple of cousins thought Louisa had worn a ring, but nobody could describe it for sure. In the end it was left up to Thomas to decide, and he remembered only the pearl."

Therese could imagine the hopelessness of trying to get them all to agree on their memories of a specific painting. "But wasn't Beatrice satisfied?" she asked.

Milo touched her chin lightly. "You're looking very lovely today," he said. "Did I already tell you that?"

She smiled. "Try to concentrate. What about Beatrice?"

"Beatrice," he said softly, "remembered emeralds."

Therese was surprised. "Emeralds?"

"She remembered emeralds." He caressed her chin again, then leaned down and set the lightest of kisses on her lips. Therese felt warm color moving up into her cheeks, and she was pleased. It was faintly erotic to have him talking about one thing but using his body to show her he was thinking about something else. As she was.

"Emeralds?" she encouraged him when he lifted his head.

His eyes focused on her lips, and his own lips twisted slightly in a maddening hint of a smile. "A matching necklace and ring set, just like the set Thomas had recently given his new bride."

Her eyebrows lifted. "Do I detect a certain amount of envy at work?"

"Envy or not," Milo said, "Beatrice claimed that she remembered emeralds in the portrait of Louisa and that Thomas had taken them to give to his wife."

Therese gave a low whistle. "Not a very friendly accusation to make."

"Beatrice was not very popular after that," Milo agreed. "I like it when you whistle."

She smiled, but didn't whistle again, even when he pursed his lips as if to encourage her.

"You can't do it, can you?" she said.

"Never could. Care to teach me?"

She licked her lips, considering him. His gaze was locked on her mouth, so that she felt a tingling of expectation there. "Maybe later," she said, trying to sound casual.

His eyes flashed to hers. "I could teach you a trick in exchange," he said.

"Like what?"

He leaned back slightly, his eyes smoldering, and she felt a tightening in her gut.

"So," she said, her voice unusually low. She swallowed. "That's why Beatrice wanted the painting back so badly, isn't it?" she went on more brightly. "It was really a matter of pride, a matter of a family feud. Is that why Thomas sent that man last night?"

Milo braced himself against the bridge railing and slid his hands into his trousers pockets. "He was evasive when I called him this morning, but I'm certain of it. Aside from the emeralds, which are priceless, Thomas's entire reputation is wrapped up with this picture. People have always been puzzled by Madame Sophie's will, and some of the cousins believe Thomas may have actually stolen the painting."

Therese stretched one leg out before her, cocking her toes to ease the stiffness in her ankle.

"Well," she said. "Thomas seemed ready enough to steal it last night."

"Beatrice was afraid of this. Thomas definitely knows something about it that he doesn't want discovered."

"Like a ring, maybe?" She thought suddenly of the clover-shaped patch on Louisa's hand.

"Yes."

She could tell Milo was watching her closely. He must have been intensely interested when she first showed him the patch on Louisa's finger, but he hadn't revealed it that day when they'd stood in the closet together with the ultraviolet light. He was willing for the restoration to proceed at a normal pace. But now Therese was curious.

"Maybe my father knew something about Thomas," she said. "Maybe that's the missing piece."

"It could be," Milo said. "I've never been able to understand why your father didn't bring the portrait of

Louisa back to Beatrice. It just doesn't make sense. Knowing your father, he could have gotten that painting out of Romania fifteen years ago, if he'd wanted to. But for some reason, after going to the effort of finding it for Beatrice, Harry chose to leave it behind. Why?"

Therese twined her fingers together, frowning. "Where did you find it?"

"About fifty miles from the mansion where I'd left your father that night. Somehow he made it to one of the neighboring homes. According to the man I met there, his parents harbored your father for a month while he recovered and he gave them the picture out of gratitude. Your father didn't tell them how valuable it was. The current owner had the picture in the kitchen of his hunting lodge in the mountains. I was very, very lucky."

"My dad must have been crazy, leaving it like that," she said. "And it doesn't make sense. He would have been incredibly protective of this painting."

"No," Milo said. "Considering the times, it was probably the best way to ensure it would be lost again, and he was determined to keep it away from Beatrice."

Therese shook her head, frowning. "I just don't know. You have to remember, Milo, how my father felt about art. The picture of Louisa is uniquely compelling. Dad must have been incredibly vulnerable to its beauty, almost as if he'd fallen in love with it. I don't know if that helps, but it's true."

"Maybe the answer is that simple," he said. "Your father did love this painting. Incidentally, I know why."

She licked her lips, looking over at him, waiting.

"Louisa looks like you," he said quietly.

She tilted her head back and laughed. "No," she said. "I don't look anything like her."

He tossed a stick in the stream below them, then turned deliberately to face her. She folded her arms across her chest and looked up at him, and what she saw tugged at her inexplicably. Milo had changed in the brief six weeks she'd known him; she could almost see it in the thick unruliness of his short hair. His entire body seemed more alive, somehow, as if he'd given up his stiff formality when he'd set his normal work on hold. Now, he had a loose-limbed grace, a barely contained energy that highlighted his innate magnetism. It was as if the change in seasons had been happening to him, peeling away the gloom and trouble of winter for the percolating optimism of spring. She couldn't help hoping that part of his change was due to her. He seemed, she thought, well—he seemed *happier*. And now he was comparing her to a girl of supermodel beauty.

"It's not the exact resemblance I mean," he was saying. "I'm talking about the more elusive quality. You know the magical thing that happens with Louisa as you back away? How her beauty just leaps out at you? And then you can't look enough? It's the same with you, Therese, only stronger."

She could feel the rush of warmth up her cheeks. "Milo," she began.

He leaned nearer, dropping his voice to an intimate pitch that made the open space of the park recede into the background.

"What can I do, Therese? I can't pretend it isn't happening. I think about you all the time. And now, after last night, I want to be with you all the time. I've never been good about my obsessions." He smiled lazily, his eyes warm and sexy. "I always give in to them."

She swallowed hard and tried to control her inner butterflies. He moved closer, stopping only when the front of his leather coat met her right elbow. His eyes, his lips, were only inches away.

"So I'm just one in a series of obsessions?" she asked. The idea stung more than she believed it could.

His eyebrows lowered slightly. "You, Therese, are my last obsession."

She laughed quickly and pivoted away from him to break the spell of his nearness. He might more accurately say she was his most recent obsession. It was the same thing, she thought. He fell into step beside her as they continued their walk through the park.

"You don't believe me?" he asked.

"No, I believe you," she said. "At least, I believe you believe what you're saying."

"But you don't trust me."

She dug her hands into the triangular pockets of her jacket. "What can I say, Milo? To be honest, you frighten me. You're so intense. How do I know you won't be interested in some other obsession next week?"

He paused, and she was forced to stop too, to turn and look at him.

"You can't believe that," he said.

She felt a brittle ache inside her and concentrated on her boots, digging one pointed toe into the gravel. She didn't know what to believe. She'd woken up a different woman, in a world where all the colors had shifted, and when she looked closely at her feelings, she was both exultant and terrified. Nobody had ever seen as deeply into her soul as he had last night, and he'd shared one of his most private memories with her. Yet there had been no spoken exchange of love. She couldn't keep the hollowness from echoing inside her, and that was what bewildered and hurt her.

"I don't know what to believe," she said. "Is that so wrong?"

She felt him step nearer, then gently grasp her elbows to guide her against his body until they were face-to-face, and his eyes devoured her with a silky hunger that made her knees shaky. She leaned against him, and that was all it took.

His lips met hers, pure desire finding its match. A certain weightlessness set in, lifting her toward him, and the fire she'd felt with him the night before was kindled again in her depths. Even with their jackets on, her body knew the tugging magnetism of his, and she responded, relishing the feel of him in the clean sunlight, as if he were part of the wind and air, surrounding and invading her.

She gasped, freeing herself, and sought his eyes to see if they confirmed that he was already as aroused as she was. He answered by kissing her again.

A group of teenagers on a basketball court started to hoot and whistle.

She laughed, backing up half a pace. "We can't do this here," she said, bracing a hand on his sleeve to steady herself.

"Then let's go home."

She shook her head, arching her eyebrows. "I have a job, remember?"

He shook his head and made a disapproving expression with his mouth. "You can resist me," he said. "This is not a good sign."

She lightly punched his arm. "Milo!"

He smiled ruefully. "I know. But this means I won't see you again until tomorrow night. I have to take Beatrice and Veronique out tonight, so I won't be at the studio. The police called and told me the person with the telescope moved out of the apartment across the street, so I think Thomas has backed off. For now. You'll be safe with Bert there in any case."

He took her hand and linked it inside his elbow, and they reluctantly traced their steps back toward the museum. The fresh wind blew at their backs, and Therese tried to memorize the moment. Soon it would be full spring, but for now the grass was still brown and matted, and a few old leaves were pressed hard in the dried mud. They passed a walled rose garden, and she looked longingly through the locked gate, wishing she and Milo had time to go there, even with no roses in bloom. It reminded her that they had no promise of a future together, and the idea made her pensive. If all she could be was his obsession for the moment, was that so bad? If an affair was all she could have with him, wasn't it still better than nothing?

In silence they traversed the paths, then crossed the arching bridge and climbed the gentle slope to the museum. She looked up at the great gray building and for the first time felt a reluctance to go inside. Always before she had been eager to go to work, privately rejoicing in how much she loved her job. Today it seemed like just work, something that kept her from doing what she really wanted to do. Her fingers instinctively tightened on Milo's elbow.

"I thought of something," she said. "Is the Orrin from your story the same as sculptor Orrin du Bois?"

Milo nodded. "He exhibited his sculptures at the opening of my first art gallery. That's what launched his career."

She tilted her face and smiled. "It didn't hurt your gallery much either, I presume."

He laughed. "No, it was profitable for everyone concerned. He doesn't have to paint houses on the side anymore, that's for sure."

"What ever happened to his 'high-spirited' daughter, the one who fell off the ladder?"

"Alvina? She married and has a couple of wild kids of her own now. She never learned to paint either."

Alvina, Therese thought. So he'd named his galleries after a wild-hearted slip of a girl. She liked the idea. It made her smile.

Milo smiled back. "Are we still on for tomorrow night?"

"You mean, the date where I don't have to pay for my half of the check?"

He grinned and gave her shoulder a squeeze. "Unless you want to," he said.

She smiled widely and reached up to kiss him quickly on the lips.

He caught her suddenly and kept her near, and she could see the flashing warmth in the way he looked at her. "I think what you really meant was this," he said huskily. And this time when their lips met, she was left shaking and empty with need, so that it was near torture to walk away from the man and go into her work.

"Holy macaroli," she whispered. She pushed through the glass doors, still in a bit of a daze. "That man is serious trouble."

The rest of the day at the museum was hectic, and Therese survived it on high-strung energy and coffee. The museum director's enthusiasm for a newly arrived triptych from Germany had him bouncing off the studio walls, bringing in every curator, benefactor, and art historian who happened to be in the museum. The triptych had arrived a month ahead of schedule, and it was truly magnificent, an elaborate, gory medieval trio of panels that spanned a good twenty feet across.

Usually Therese would have been enraptured, but for once she saw the triptych merely as so much work she was going to have to try to fit in, when she was already stretched too thin. Mickey wanted her to begin the restoration immediately, and she had to remind him twice of the projects she already had going. There was an implicit expectation that she would come in to work overtime, and she was certain Mickey had forgotten she was working for Milo in her off hours. She didn't remind him.

She tried to fit into her old, obsessively driven groove, but something in her had expanded, made her impatient with her work, as if she couldn't put her face against the magnifying glass close enough to focus anymore. All she could think of was Milo, and his last riveting kiss, and how much she longed to see him again. Could she really survive thirty hours until their date? What did it mean that she longed to be with him, yet was afraid of him when she was? She wanted to believe he was falling in love with her, but he never used those words. And what did love mean to Milo, anyway? For her, love meant a future with someone, passion and daily life combined, dreams and solid earth all in one person. Maybe she was idealistic. Maybe in the real world love like that didn't exist. But deep inside she wanted to believe, and that was what frightened her most.

Later that night, as Bert dozed by the desk with a book on parenting spread on his knees, Therese labored over the portrait of Louisa and tried not to think of Milo too much.

She had already meticulously surface-cleaned the painting to remove the layer of soot, gently wiping with cotton swabs and a mild enzymatic solution. Then she'd removed the yellowed natural-resin varnish with another solvent. Now she was concentrating on the overpainted areas, the islands of black that had shown up so vividly under the ultraviolet light. She could clearly see the overpaint on Louisa's hand, and she hoped the varnish beneath it had protected the original paint underneath. Tonight she was undermining the overpaint by carefully solubilizing it, putting her face near and squinting with the concentration of an eye surgeon.

"Oh, my gosh!" she whispered. She nearly went cross-eyed with amazement.

Beneath the flesh-colored overpaint on Louisa's finger was a darker band of mauve and green—hints of shadow and a jewel. It was a ring, she thought. An emerald ring! The original painting had a ring! Milo was going to be thrilled.

She let out a choked whooping sound. And then, with a shock, an old nursery rhyme popped into her head:

> Pity the oyster that hides no pearl
> For searching greed will destroy it as well.

Her mind went still and cold as the words circled through her mind again, as if called back from beyond the grave, a whisper in her father's voice. It sounded like a nursery rhyme, she thought, but it wasn't. None of her friends had ever known it. It was a rhyme her father had told her countless times, until it became an accepted quirk of her heritage. But he must have made it up himself. Now suddenly it fit. This was the memory! she thought, as her excitement expanded again. This was the message from her father. But what did it mean?

Resuming her work, she bent over the ring patch again and meticulously removed the last of the overpaint and the layer of old varnish. It took hours, but she worked with a passion that made it seem like minutes, and by dawn there it was: a perfect setting of two little emeralds and one larger one, as pretty and dainty as Louisa herself.

"There," she whispered, sitting back to admire the picture as a whole. It made sense now, the position of that left hand folded on top of the right. There was a shimmering promise in that ring, and youthful pride. Therese would bet anything that it had been an engagement ring to Louisa from her betrothed.

But why had it been covered? When and by whom? It

could have been before or after her father had hid with the painting in that wine cellar.

Milo would be so happy, she thought. But it was five in the morning. She'd have to wait. She could get up before work and tell him face-to-face. She smiled and propped a protective covering over the painting.

Only when she stood up did she realize how exhausted she was. Every muscle in her back and shoulders was stiff, and her knees were so cramped, she could hardly keep her balance. She'd been up for nearly twenty-four hours straight, and the strain of weeks of effort was finally catching up with her.

She'd just go home for a little sleep, she thought. Just a catnap. Then that night, after her date with Milo, she'd sleep like a dog.

But by the time she reached her nearby apartment, she was sagging, and the shower that was supposed to invigorate her left her semicomatose. She slid on her terry bathrobe, took two steps toward the coffeemaker, and did an about-face flat onto her bed.

When she finally awoke, it was to the sound of the door buzzer, not her alarm clock. Disoriented and sleepy-eyed, she sat up and checked the clock. "Four!" she gasped, jumping out of bed. "Four in the afternoon!"

She'd missed going to see Milo. She'd missed going to work. She'd missed practically the entire day.

"Oh, my gosh!" she squealed. She wrapped her bathrobe tightly around herself, bolted down the stairs, and pulled open the door just as another imperious knock came from outside.

Milo Dansforth stood in the full-blown orange of the late-afternoon sunlight, his favorite coat unbuttoned and his collar askew, as if he was in a hurry. He looked so incredibly handsome that it was all she could do not to throw herself into his arms.

"So you are here," he said, sounding satisfied with himself. "Are you sick?"

Therese pulled her bathrobe tighter at the collar, keenly aware that beneath the soft terry she was still naked, and gestured him in.

"No, I just overslept," she said. She grinned shyly. "A lot, actually. What are you doing here?"

"When I called for you at the museum, Mickey said it was the first time you'd ever missed a day of work, so I came by to see if you were all right."

"Mickey? Oh, my gosh. Was he mad?"

Milo laughed, pulling the door closed behind him. "He said it was about time."

The entryway of Therese's duplex was so narrow, Milo had to twist his shoulders to pass the two mailboxes. Therese backed up the first step, then turned to lead the way. She pulled a hand through her hair, feeling acutely unprepared. Milo had never come inside her apartment before, and she hadn't had a chance to get ready. She must look a mess, with her uncombed hair and sleepy eyes. And what would he think of her place? She hadn't had time to clean up at all.

She closed the door to her bedroom before he could look in, then led him into the living room. Glancing sideways at him, she hoped he didn't think the room looked too strange.

Her living room was in the front quadrant of the

apartment and it faced south and west, with enormous windows on both sides. The afternoon light streaked in almost sideways as the low sun headed toward the city-scape horizon to the right. She had painted the walls a creamy white, the ceiling a soft blue, with an intricate border at the top of the walls in indigo and brown and gold. The floor was made of wide pine boards, worn to a golden, satiny finish that always felt delicious to her bare feet, so delicious she'd never covered it with a carpet. The only two pieces of furniture in the room were an upright piano against the north wall and a great double-seated rocker with thick, inviting cushions on its seat and back, as if someone had taken a porch swing and cheated gravity by setting it on the huge curving rockers. Therese loved to cuddle up in that rocker and lean her head back, and she asked for no more serene place on earth. She could spend hours there, simply gazing out the windows, or consuming a romantic novel, or writing in her journal. But she knew the room seemed peculiar to her friends, who had a habit of coming with folding chairs when she invited them over for company. She didn't care.

Though there was no other furniture, the walls of the room were densely hung with photos, watercolors, and oil paintings of all sizes and subjects. There was a small watercolor of a boat race off Madeline Island, a large oil painting of a field of lilacs, and another oil of the St. Croix River Valley that had once hung in her grandparents' home. There were black-and-white photos of children from Brazil, and a series of photos of a clay bowl being thrown on a wheel. There were more paintings of a bullfighter, a tractor, a giant seashell, and an abstract work that reminded her of stained-glass irises. Therese had many favorites, but the one she loved most was a small watercolor of a dark-haired girl walking in a garden, lush with reds and greens and brilliant yellows. Her father had given her that painting on her thirteenth birthday, and she still loved to imagine herself in that garden, with her father waiting for her just around the corner. She knew, hidden on the back of the frame, was an inscription from him: "I love my darling Therese more than three full moons. Happy Birthday."

Milo had stepped into the room and stopped beside the rocker, turning slowly to take in all of the paintings and photographs. As she watched him, she saw his face register surprise, then appreciation, then a curious mix of sorrow and longing. Finally he smiled, a small, wistful smile.

"Why didn't you tell me?" he asked.

"Tell an art dealer that I have a few paintings?" She shook her head. "This is a very private collection."

"But you have a fortune on your walls," he said. "You could buy a home three times the size of your apartment if you sold just a few of them."

"Why? What would I do with more space? I'd only want to hang more pictures, and this is all I can afford at the moment."

Milo was watching her with unguarded amazement. "You're incredible," he said.

She laughed. "Yeah. That's why I just overslept a whole day. Do you think you could make yourself at home while I clean up?"

He took his coat off and set it on the back of the rocker. His eyes grew warmly appreciative as he took in her bathrobe, her unruly hair. "Looks like you already got cleaned up," he said.

She curled her arms around herself, smiling. "You're supposed to overlook my disarray."

"Like you overlooked my disarray that first morning in the studio?"

Her mind flashed back to the morning she'd found him in his black sweatpants and nothing more. A slow burn crept into her cheeks. "Something like that," she said.

He grinned.

Feeling both shy and exhilarated, Therese backed out of the doorway and headed into her little kitchen. "Would you make us a quick pot of coffee?" she asked as Milo followed her. "I haven't gotten groceries lately, but I think there's enough coffee left." She peeked in her freezer and took out a bag of coffee beans. It rattled when she shook it. "From my aunt's plantation," she said, looking over at him to see if he was cooperating. "There's a grinder behind the toaster."

Sunlight slanted in the little window over the sink, illuminating the dishwashing liquid and a small Venetian vase she kept on the sill. The blue and white checks on the counter and floor brought a hint of country charm to the city kitchen. It smelled faintly of red peppers and chocolate, spice and sweetness, and she realized she'd missed having time to cook slow, savory dinners for herself.

Milo took the bag of coffee beans and reached for the grinder. "I like your kitchen," he said.

"Thanks." She was about to offer to make him dinner sometime, but then she realized she didn't know how long he'd be around. An awkward silence stretched out, and the reality of the situation hit Therese with sudden clarity: Milo Dansforth was standing in her kitchen, holding a bag of coffee beans, looking both domestic and exotic at the same time. Her gaze was focused inexplicably on his nicely shaped fingernails, and she was finding it hard to breathe. Something was missing, something like a kiss. And yet the mood was wrong for her to lean forward and settle herself in his arms. She groped for something to say that would relieve the unspoken tension.

"Have you seen Louisa?" she asked.

Milo smiled and lifted his fingertips in a gesture of perfection. "I came straight from the studio," he said. "It's incredible. Absolutely incredible."

"I think so too," she said, clasping her hands together. "I've never seen anything like it. Beatrice's ring! Did you tell her yet?"

"I wanted to talk to you first."

"She's going to be thrilled," Therese said. Then why did her heart suddenly constrict with dread? She forced herself to seem enthusiastic. "It's just what she was hoping for. She'll finally get even with her wicked cousin."

Milo laughed. "You like the idea of revenge, don't you?"

"Justice," she corrected him. "She'll finally get justice, after all these years."

He nodded slowly, and Therese tipped her face, watching him, sensing some hesitance in him.

"Aren't you glad?" she asked.

"Of course I am," he said quickly. "Let's go celebrate."

She turned toward the doorway. "I'll only be a minute. There's a stereo on top of the refrigerator, if you want music." She pointed helpfully. "And the cups are over the microwave."

He smiled. "I'll find things."

But she was certain that something had changed. Whether it was because the ring had been discovered or because Milo was finally standing in her own space, something had changed. In the whole fifteen minutes since he'd entered her apartment, he hadn't made one move to kiss her.

SEVEN

When she twirled into her bedroom to get dressed, Therese couldn't help remembering again the first time she'd met Milo in the studio. That time he'd been the one to take a shower while she waited; now their situations were reversed. She decided on a superquick shower to freshen up after her sleep, and went into the bathroom. She pulled the curtain back with a squeak of plastic rings. The water came on with stinging force and she tipped her head back under the spray, letting the droplets course over her face and down her body. Slipping the bar of soap up her arm, she felt her body tingle with heightened awareness. She'd never been this delighted about a date before, and her expectation added pleasure to even the simplest things, like the warm roughness of her big towel and the plush thickness of the rug under her toes when she stepped out.

She used another towel to twist around her hair while she dug her blow-dryer out of a drawer. She blasted it at the mirror to clear the fog, then brushed and dried her hair, wondering for the millionth time if she should cut it. The satiny black mass fell almost to her elbows and was slippery as water once it was dry. It took her only another minute to twist her hair into a shiny knot that bared the back of her neck. No braid for her tonight, she thought, smiling.

She pulled her red sheath dress over her head and paused, listening. At first she thought Milo had turned on the stereo, then she realized he must be playing the piano. She listened, curious, as he cautiously played several bars of a Bach sonata she'd kept in the piano bench, going slowly as if he were searching out the notes. The melody was familiar, and though broken by his hesitations, it lost none of its lilting musicality. When he went back to the opening to start again, the melody came through more surely the second time. She smiled to herself as she did up her zipper, pleased to realize he must have learned to play once and even more pleased that he felt comfortable enough to play her old upright.

Silver earrings dangled daintily from her earlobes, brushing her skin with faint coolness when she turned her face to the mirror. She pressed her lips together, then opened them to apply a bold hue of red. Next she used her eyeliner, leaning close to the mirror and touching the pencil to the corner of her eyelid with the same exacting accuracy she used at work. All the while the searching notes came from the piano in the living room. She dropped a string of black beads around her neck, moved back to test the effect, and frowned critically at herself.

Let me do the Cinderella thing for once, she thought. *Let me, this one night, be irresistibly beautiful, even if I don't have a fairy godmother.*

Her wish must have been answered, for when she stepped into the living room, Milo turned from the piano and literally did a double take. She smiled shyly, pleased at his speechless reaction.

"You like red, don't you?" she asked. Her slim, close-fitting, long-sleeved dress was one graceful line from shoulder to just below her knee, simple yet subtly accentuating her feminine curves.

He cleared his throat. "I do."

"Is it too much? Are we doing drive-through?"

He shook his head slowly. "Not anymore."

She laughed. She felt like a goddess, powerful and alluring.

"I didn't know you played the piano," she said.

"I don't. I haven't for a million years. My mother made me take lessons when I was a kid."

"But you still remember how to play?"

"I guess I do. Enough to pick out the notes. Will you play for me?"

She shook her head, an emphatic no. "I'm an awful player. Everyone tells me so. No sense of rhythm whatsoever. But I do love it. I go through periods when I play every night. Then I won't touch it for six months. Sad, don't you think?"

Milo laughed quietly and stood up. "Not sad. Genuine."

She lifted her chin slightly, watching him. "Or lazy. I'd guess you're too much of a perfectionist to do something at all unless you can master it."

"Something like that," he said, his words an echo of her own from earlier. Their language was beginning to have a history to it.

She gazed at him, considering. Perhaps he had to master everything he encountered, she thought, a faint shiver passing through her. She'd thought she was getting to know Milo fairly well, but she could see she'd only begun to plumb his depths. He intrigued her, yet at the same time she was increasingly certain they needed more time. Time was something they might not have, now that she'd found the emeralds on Louisa's hand.

Standing against the backdrop of her art collection, Milo looked out of scale, too large and three-dimensional in her small, solitary home, as if one of her paintings had come to life and wouldn't fit back into its frame. And she was vaguely aware that her home had made her seem more three-dimensional to him, too, since every picture, every object, even her coffee related to her heritage, her past. A history that he had only begun to learn about.

"I'd still like to hear you play sometime," he said.

She shook her head again, backing toward the doorway. "I have to be in the mood. Or completely indifferent to my audience."

His eyebrows lifted, and he crossed the room to her. "That's not an option," he said.

"No," she replied. "I guess not."

He stopped before her and she could feel his gaze traveling from her eyes to her neck, then down the length of her dress, so that his face was lowered and she itched to run her fingers through his hair.

"I like this dress," he said, glancing back up. "Even better than your jeans."

She felt her face grow warm, remembering how he'd taken her jeans off when he'd made love to her two nights before. And still he made no move to touch her. A wary, hungry light glimmered in his watchful eyes, and she took an infinitesimal step closer to him, so they were practically touching but not. His eyelids lowered slightly, and she could feel the warmth of his breath touch her lips, and still he didn't move. A strange coiling of desire curled through her, combined with a subtle sense of danger, as if she acknowledged she was playing a game of temptation, seeing how far she could take it before he had to give in and claim her. Because that was what she wanted, she realized. She wanted him to need her, wanted him to reach out for her first, and until he did, she would remain elusively near.

His eyes had darkened to mere slits. She saw him ball his hands into fists and slide them into his trousers pockets.

"Did you want that coffee?" he asked with forced casualness.

"I don't, after all. Do you?"

He shook his head, muttering something that sounded like "Damn the coffee," but she couldn't be sure.

She smiled, looking up at him sideways through her lashes. "Shall we go then?"

He stepped back slightly, breaking the tension between them. "Sure," he said.

She took a moment to turn off the coffee machine and the lights, pick up her purse and coat. She slipped on her coat before he could offer to help her, then she jingled her keys. "All ready," she said, and let him go down the stairs before her so that she could lock the door. Milo held the outside door for her, and she stepped out onto the porch.

She shivered, because the early evening air had turned cooler. The last of the sunset was stretched across the sky, splashing a wash of orange and purple above the duplexes on the opposite side of the street.

"You need to keep your neck warm," he said, and before she was aware of his intention, he pulled the cashmere scarf from his own neck and wrapped it around hers. The soft fabric was already warm as it touched her skin, but it sent a shiver down her neck. She reached and curled her fingers in the soft wool. He still hadn't touched her. If anything, he'd been careful to keep his fingers away even as he'd set the scarf around her neck. But she thought she knew why, or at least she hoped she did. If he ever did touch her, he wouldn't be able to stop.

"Thanks," she said.

"My pleasure."

A few hours later, at the end of a leisurely dinner, Therese leaned back in her plush seat and smiled, curling her arms around herself. Their waiter took away the remains of her chicken marsala just after she finished the last butter-rich bite.

She glanced around the restaurant, where well-dressed diners filled every chair in the expensively appointed room. The chandeliers were set for a dim, intimate light and candles glowed on each table. She and Milo were sitting in a booth, slightly raised above the main floor, so she could see across to where a pianist sat at a baby grand, playing old Gershwin and Berlin tunes, romantic melodies evoking an earlier time.

"Are you sure you planned this before you knew I liked the piano?" she asked.

He smiled. "Is that so strange?"

"I guess not. Now, if only they had one of those little dessert carts, this place would be perfect."

"Well," Milo said slowly, "you can choose something if you like. But I called this morning to request a certain dessert and I was assured the chef would prepare it for us."

"You didn't," she said.

His teeth showed in an infectious grin, even as two slices of cheesecake with chocolate-cookie-crumb crust appeared with their coffee.

"I couldn't be more touched if you baked it yourself," Therese said.

He laughed. "I can only go so far."

She slid the first forkful of the light, sweet dessert into her mouth and closed her eyes at the melting pleasure.

"Wow," she said reverently.

He silently passed over his own plate, and she laughed, accepting it.

"You know that photograph at the top of your stairs, beside the blue vase?" he asked. "Who are all those people? Your family? I meant to ask before."

She looked up at him, surprised, then swallowed her cheesecake. "I have zillions of cousins in St. Paul, Minnesota, and São Paulo, Brazil. Great coincidence, isn't it? We have reunions every couple of years, and that was the latest in Brazil."

He leaned back and fingered his water goblet. "What about your grandparents? Do they still live in St. Paul?"

She ate another bite of cheesecake, preparing the

words in her mind before she said them aloud. "They died with my father. The three of them were driving out west on a vacation and their car got hit by an RV. It was head-on, at close to sixty miles an hour. No one survived."

Milo's face was grave with concern. "I didn't realize your grandparents were in the same crash. I'm so sorry."

She looked away. "I try not to think about it," she said quietly. "There was nothing anybody could do."

Her gaze shifted to the glass globe on the table that flickered with a votive candle. The shadows looked warm, and she spread her fingers toward the light. There was no way for her to explain the loneliness of that first winter without her father or grandparents. She'd struggled just to get up in the morning, to get out the door and go to her classes. Josh had died only the year before, and then to lose her father and grandparents . . . It had been more than she could handle at first. But five years had passed since then, and she'd grown to accept what she couldn't change. The picture of Louisa had brought a new peace into her life too.

"A.K. was a big help," she said. "He kept checking on me. I'll always be grateful to him for that. And my extended family has always been there for me."

"But still," Milo said.

She nodded, feeling the quiet solitude in her heart, the simple faith that had kept her going. She closed her eyes and lowered her chin, then looked up again and gave a small smile.

"They're with me still, of course," she said. "Something my father used to say to me came back just yesterday, a memory I might have lost forever if you hadn't hired me to work on Louisa."

Milo's expression became curious. "What was that?"

"An old saying. 'Pity the oyster that hides no pearl, for searching greed will destroy it as well.' It popped into my mind the instant I found the emeralds."

Milo was instantly alert. "What do you think it means?"

She shrugged. "I don't know. I always thought it meant that innocent things can get damaged if they're in the way when a rough, greedy person comes through."

"But how does that apply to Louisa?"

Therese frowned and sat back. "I don't know. I thought at first it might be important, but I don't see how it could be."

A distracted, puzzled expression crossed Milo's face and he glanced across the room. The pianist finished one song and started another at a quicker tempo, and Therese felt a vague sense of fear or uncertainty.

"Milo?" she asked.

He shook his head. "You must be right. But it's odd, isn't it?"

She laughed. "I'm used to things being odd. Around you."

He smiled at her. The warm light returned to his eyes, and she felt a sweet, crumbling feeling inside. For long moments neither of them spoke, and Therese soaked in the silence they shared, feeling the bond that let them be comfortable with each other even during a pause. But it wasn't pure comfort she felt. The subdued tension, like spun energy, was there between them, too, as tangible as the table.

Her gaze fell again on the little candle, and she bumped her finger along the ridges in the glass. Milo kept his hand resting on the table, a few inches from her own, and she wondered if he would reach out and touch her fingers.

"You know, there's a theory about hurricanes," he said, his voice low and beguiling. "It has to do with weather patterns."

"What's this theory?"

"It's the Improbable Hurricane Theory."

"You're making this up. You always make things up."

"I'm not," he said, his eyebrows lifting. "It goes like this. You watch the isobars, looking for patterns." He traced imaginary lines on the tablecloth with one long finger. "Then you get all the computers to try to predict a specific hurricane. You control for the seasons, the tides, the gulfstream." His smile became more quizzical. "The migrations of whales. You think you have it all figured out. You say, the hurricane will hit on this day, in this location. Then you see one coming. You're delighted at first because you were hoping you were right. But then it's a *hurricane*. Havoc and mayhem rampage through your life, turning everything upside down, even your stomach. You can't sleep. You can't find your batteries. Your ears are always listening and—get this—your ankles tingle."

She watched him, trying to gauge how serious he was. His face was sober, but there was a telltale light in his eye, half wicked, half expectant.

"What I don't understand," he said, "is why do your ankles tingle?"

"Do I sense a metaphor here?" she asked.

His eyes became very serious, and a flicker of reflected light from the candle emphasized their depths. "I think I've been hit."

Therese was totally unprepared for the tumult of emotions that whipped through her. She licked her lips, speechless, and struggled to believe she was really hearing this. He was *not* talking about a hurricane anymore, that was for sure. She had the most awful premonition that he was about to produce a jeweler's box, but his hand remained motionless on the table and he simply waited, watching her.

When she still didn't respond, his eyes shifted slightly and she could see he was staring beyond her into space, just for an instant.

"Perhaps we'll explore the subtleties of the theory later," he said casually.

Too casually. She had the horrible certainty he was hurt and that compounded her confusion. She was relieved when the waiter came up right then with the check.

Milo began a patter of small talk that was completely foreign to her. He'd never talked in such a polite, impersonal way with her, but while it puzzled her, she was also grateful, for it got them smoothly out of the restaurant and into his car. Once Milo started driving, he fell silent, and Therese watched the night pass by her window as the car progressed down the streets.

When he took the turn that started them toward his house, she felt a new surge of emotion, part fear, part expectation. They were going to have a chance to talk this out then, she thought. So why was she afraid?

He pulled up in front of his house and turned off the engine.

"You'll come in for a moment, won't you?" he asked.

"I'd like to," she said.

He came around quickly to open her door, and she preceded him up the walkway and into the house. Milo flipped on the small lamp in the foyer, then leaned back to close the front door. Therese jumped at the thumping noise, all her senses becoming hyperaware. In the silence she swore she could hear her own heart beating.

"Milo . . ." she began.

"What?"

She licked her lips, trying to voice a question that would let him know the turmoil in her heart. But she was frightened. And she didn't know what to do about the hungry, possessive look on his face.

He came a step nearer, then another, until they were no more than an inch apart. He seemed to be asking for something from her, but she didn't know what it was. All she knew was that she wanted to be in his arms.

He gave her one more long, penetrating look, then whispered a curse and pulled her into his arms. Finally she felt his mouth against hers. Keys and coats dropped to the floor as he urged her nearer, kissing her with a reckless hunger that took her breath away. She ran her fingers up into his hair, feeling the residual coolness in the short strands, then forgetting everything as his fingers removed the scarf he'd loaned her and his kiss moved to her throat, to the pulse below her jaw.

Her eyes closed, but her other senses more than made up for her sweet blindness. Smooth strokes along her back, warm through the delicate fabric of her dress, had her toes curling with pleasure. The sound of his uneven breathing made her own breathing short. The last chill from his clothing was a kind of smell all its own, and his kiss, when it returned to her waiting lips, had a taste unlike anything she'd ever known.

"Milo," she whispered.

"My God, Therese." He hugged her close, nestling his face against her hair. "You have no idea what you do to me."

He leaned away so he could look into her eyes, and what she saw in his face made her heart expand in her chest. Love and desire radiated from his features, beckoning to her, and she could feel her last resistance crumbling. He found her hand at his waist and captured it in his, lifting it to his lips.

"My hurricane," he teased gently. He tugged at her hand, leading her farther into the house. "I want to show you something."

"What?"

He took her around a corner and switched on the lights in a small, book-lined library. Three of the walls had built-in shelves that were filled with hardcovers, small sculptures, and a curious collection of teapots. The fourth wall had a fireplace, and on the mantel, below a large mirror, was a row of more teapots, large and small, some conspicuously old and others new. Therese was enchanted.

"What a lovely room," she said. "Those teapots are amazing."

"I had them sent over from my place in Paris," he said.

"They're yours?" she asked, surprised. She had thought the furnishings of the house came with his rental agreement.

He laughed. "I thought they'd make it feel more like home."

Something in his voice made her pause just as she was about to pick up a small yellow teapot. He was looking through a couple of papers on his desk, then he found the one he wanted.

"Here. Take a look," he said.

She accepted the paper from his hand and began to read a dense legal document. She'd only read the first sentence before her eyes scanned down the rest of the page, instantly understanding, even though she'd never seen a real estate purchasing agreement before. Her breathing, her heartbeat, everything inside her seemed to slow down, even stop.

"I'm buying the house," he said, smiling.

"*This* house?" she asked, shocked.

He walked around the desk, still smiling. "You said you liked it. I like it too. All it needs are a few more teapots. Maybe a painting or two."

Her mind refused to budge. "You're buying this house?" she repeated. "But you live in Paris!"

"Did live in Paris," he said softly.

His hands grasped her arms. She closed her eyes, shaking her head. Every instinct in her told her to flee, yet her bones were melting again in the maddening way they did whenever he touched her.

"I thought you'd be glad," he said.

She opened her eyes, because she detected the stilted note in his voice that meant she'd hurt him.

"I am glad," she said. "But, Milo. This means you're going to stay."

He didn't look surprised. "That's the idea," he said.

She couldn't stand to be so near to him, not when her heart was beating so wildly. Pulling away, she circled around a chair, putting some space between them.

Milo crossed his arms over his chest and frowned, studying her. "Okay, so you aren't exactly ecstatic. Still, I didn't expect raw horror. Maybe you'd care to explain."

She gripped the back of the chair as tight as she could and sledgehammered her thoughts into line. "Explain what?" she hedged.

"Don't do this. I need to know what's going on."

She felt a trip of fear in her heart. It was time to be honest, no matter what it sounded like. "At first I was holding back because I knew you could leave at any time, and I didn't see the point of getting involved with you at all."

He nodded. "I remember. Go on."

"Then," she continued, "I allowed myself to get swept up into our affair, knowing that it would have to end when you left. Nobody's fault, just reality. I thought I could be tough enough for that, and anyway I had no choice, because I couldn't resist."

She ground her nails into the upholstery of the chair and stared at him, hoping he'd understand. Flashing memories of their night in the studio raced through her mind. He only waited, his expression becoming more and more unreadable.

"Now it turns out you aren't just some exotic, fantastic man who's ready to introduce me to the delights of . . ." She stopped in confusion and tried to refocus. "Now you want to turn this relationship into a reality," she continued. "If you move here, there's a possibility you'll stay in my life, Milo. Long-term. And that scares me."

He shoved his hands in his pockets and looked down at the floor. He was silent so long, Therese's arms began to ache and she had to loosen her grip on the chair back.

" 'Some exotic, fantastic man,' " he echoed quietly.

She twisted her fingers together. "That isn't what I meant," she said. "I mean you are, but that isn't all." She groaned. She was putting it so badly.

"Then why does the idea of having me in your life long-term frighten you so much?" he asked finally, looking up. "Do you need a spoken commitment?"

"No!"

"Then what?" he persevered. "You're afraid I don't love you enough?"

The air squeezed sharply out of her lungs. He said it so easily, so absolutely, as if his love were a fact between them.

"No," she said.

"Then there's only one thing left." His eyes tensed slightly at the corners. "You don't love me back. Isn't that it?"

She lifted a beseeching hand. "It's just so soon, Milo. Josh and I knew each other all the way through high school and part of college before we were sure we belonged together."

"Am I anything like Josh?" he asked. His voice had an edge of anger to it. "Tell me. Because if I'm competing with some ghost, you have to let me know."

She shook her head. "No. You're nothing like Josh."

His eyes, from across the room, had a fierce, predatorial look. "I'd bet you a dozen paintings that you aren't much like the girl who became engaged to him either. People change, Therese. And what you and I have between us is unique to us. Don't pretend you want to know me in the way you knew Josh."

With that, she knew he had forever dismissed Josh as an issue between them.

"I—I don't," she said.

"Then say what you really mean. You think you love me, but you aren't convinced."

It sounded so cold to her, so indecisive, yet he was close to the truth.

She struggled to explain. "How can I love you when I never knew that you collect teapots? You only found out tonight that I play the piano. You have to know a person to love them fully. Why can't we just take this more slowly?"

He crossed the room to her, his eyes holding her gaze. "Because those are just external details," he said. "Because your caution is an excuse that keeps you from the truth. Because there isn't anything time can give us that I can't offer you right now." He walked around the chair and reached for her hands, pressing them in his strong, warm clasp.

"I am profoundly in love with you, Therese," he said, "and every minute that you wait to decide, I am more alone than I have ever been in my whole life."

"Oh, no," she whispered. She didn't know if she regretted the pain she caused him or if he'd at last found a way to crumble her defenses, for in that instant he kissed her with such dazzling intensity that logical thought was rendered impossible.

This time it was more than a game, more than an

experiment to see if the chemistry between them was powerful enough. She could feel that he'd raised the stakes by professing his love, and he seemed prepared to use his body and her own to try to convince her she loved him too. His kiss was molten fire, and she was locked against him, her entire body arching to deepen their kiss. She twined her fingers in his hair and felt the heat of his hands through her dress. Her belly was pressed against the hard edge of his belt buckle.

Milo lifted her slightly and she felt her weight come down on the corner of his desk. His kiss moved lower, finding the neckline of her red dress so that she could feel the heat of his breath against her sensitive skin. She closed her eyes and rested her cheek on his hair, unable to bear the surge of emotions that was crowding through her. Before she'd been curious, going on instinct, but this time she knew how to move her body and ask for his caresses, and a sensual rhythm began to beat deep in her chest.

Milo's kiss lingered at her neckline, but his hands stroked downward to where the hem of her dress was riding up her legs. With gentle, exploring fingers he worked it upward until her knees parted enough to let him slide his body between them. She became heavy and half blind with sweet desire as his palms stroked the inner skin of her thighs. He pressed his body against hers, and she lay back on the desk, sending a sheaf of papers to the floor. Her bead necklace slipped sideways around her throat and her twist of hair shifted beneath her head. Milo trailed his lips down her chest until she could feel the moist warmth of his mouth through the thin fabric of her dress and bra.

She circled her hands around to the front of him and began to work on his shirt buttons, her fingers torturously slow when she longed to feel his bare skin against her. The last button came loose with a sharp snap, and she tugged the fabric back along his shoulders, until he had to straighten and twist free of his shirt, his bare chest gleaming in the golden light of the lamp. He was the most gorgeous man she'd ever seen, toned and strong and lean, a perfect work of nature.

She half sat up to kiss his lips, then angled her head to taste the hot skin of his chest. Exotic and fantastic, she thought. He was all of it, and so much more. If she could make love with him again tonight, she knew it would be something she would never forget for as long as she lived.

She could feel him sliding the hem of her dress higher, then the exquisite sensation, both cold and hot, when his fingers found the skin above the top edges of her stockings.

He paused, and she opened her eyes to see him watching her intently, a half smile on his lips. "We've been here before," he said.

But that other time they stopped, she thought. Then, with a shock of desire, she felt his fingers tracing the edge of her panties. He lingered there, stroking and teasing until she was damp and achingly ready for him. With a small impatient movement, she shifted downward on the desk, bringing her body against his hips, where his hard arousal was pressing. She gasped at the intimate contact, yet knew she wanted more.

Milo's strong hands were sliding under and around her, pressing her body tightly against his. "Hold on," he whispered. He paused to gather his strength, then lifted her in his arms, keeping her legs straddled intimately around his waist. She pressed her lips against his neck and breathed deep, trying to keep her body in a holding pattern while he carried her upstairs and set her down beside a bed.

She had a fleeting impression of a softly lit bedroom in royal blue and burgundy, but then her focus was utterly on Milo and the possessive hunger that burned in his eyes. He reached for the hem of her dress and slid it upward, his palms taking an intimate sweep with it, past her stockings, past her panties. He paused at her waist and pulled her to him, the circle of her dress tight against her back, for a long, delving kiss. Breaking the kiss on a moan, he pulled the dress up farther, exposing her lacy bra and full, taut breasts. He slid the dress over her head and dropped it to the floor. The front clasp of her bra gave easily, releasing the constricting material, and she arched with feline grace when she felt his tongue circle the aroused peak of her breast. Her knees were growing unbearably weak, and she sucked her stomach in as tantalizing sensations spread outward from where his mouth lingered.

She murmured his name, her voice a rough plea.

He laid her back on the bed, and she felt deliciously sensual and inviting as she watched him hastily discard the rest of his clothes and then stretch out beside her, long and hot. The naked need in his eyes sent an arrow of desire through her body, and she rolled against him, gasping as her bare breasts met the warm skin of his chest and craving the feel of his arousal against her. His finger found the moist, aching part of her, and she opened her legs to him, while a helpless yearning expanded within her. Whatever sanity she still had was lost as his fingers stroked her, and she buried her face against his chest, breathing in his masculine scent. When he finally slid her panties down her legs, she rolled near to him again, unable to imagine she could wait any longer. It seemed like forever since he'd first touched her, and the agony of her need filled every particle of her being.

With steadying hands at her waist, he pulled her on top of him, then lifted a hand to the back of her neck. She felt a prickle along her scalp as he found the clasp that held her hair. She heard the slight snap, then her black hair was slipping over her shoulders, sliding forward around her face. The silky threads splayed across his chest, and he inhaled sharply. She wanted him to ache the way she did, his whole body liquid and burning, straining for release. Using the backs of her knuckles, she brushed her hands over the hard nipples of his chest and smiled with a secret sense of power when he closed his eyes and gripped her waist harder. Sitting up, she skimmed her hands down him, exploring the hard planes of his abdomen, then turning a finger in the cluster of curls at his groin. She closed her hand over his arousal and felt his body go perfectly still, as if every nerve in his body was concentrated on her touch. She encircled him slowly and stroked upward, feeling his resistance like the last beat before an explosion.

He closed a hand over hers, and a rough chuckle escaped his lips.

"We need to hold on a second," he said.

"No," she said simply. Every fiber of her being objected.

His chest rumbled with amusement. "Yes, monster." It took him only a moment to reach into the drawer next to the bed and slip on protection while she waited, watching with curious interest.

For a moment he wasn't touching her, but she still straddled him, and when his fingers sought out her intimate folds, her body was open to him and completely unable to resist. Her hips began to sway with an inner rhythm, as if he were luring her into an intricate, primal dance. She licked her lips, voicing his name, while deep inside she felt as if a dam was about to burst.

Then he was positioning himself beneath her, guiding her with a hand on her hip until she was poised above him. He rocked his hips upward, and she issued a small cry of pleasure as he entered her, her body welcoming his fullness with exquisite delight. She tipped her head back as waves of liquid heat expanded through her. Falling forward, she clutched at his shoulders, arching her back, trying to bring herself even closer.

The last thread of his control snapped. He was pure, driving energy beneath her, a sensual ride that rolled into her and captured her even as her heart burst in her chest. He gripped her thighs and thrust into her, driving himself deep, until a shattering feeling began at her inner core and spiraled outward, a crystalline explosion of ecstasy that convulsed her body. The savage upheaval went on and on, ravaging and electrifying her, until a galaxy of stars tore through her and carried her upward.

She knew he had hit his climax as he wrapped her fiercely in his arms, pinning her against him, crushing her breasts against his chest, as the last waves of ecstasy pulsed between them, hot and strong. She gripped him with equal force until she felt the weight gradually return to her body, the tingling awareness of utter pleasure sweetening every nerve from her eyebrows to her toenails and back again.

EIGHT

Therese lay in the circle of Milo's arms, cuddled close to his steadily beating heart, her cheek against his bare chest. She felt deliciously loose-limbed and relaxed as she stretched her toes down under the cover and smiled.

She gazed curiously around his bedroom, seeing details by the morning light that she'd been blind to the night before. It was a richly furnished, masculine room, with a great bay window and a narrow door that led out to a balcony. Everything was comfortable and tastefully chosen, yet the decor was disappointingly impersonal. She could see he hadn't yet changed anything there, as he had in the library with his teapot collection. The drapes had to go, she mused, erasing the heavy fabric in her mind's eye and imagining other window treatments in a lighter, warmer green.

Then her gaze fell on a little dish on the bedside table and a scrap of white paper curled inside it. Several smooth stones and a shell were in the dish too. She squinted at the scrap of paper and then it hit her. It was a fortune cookie fortune. It must be hers, she thought. He'd saved it.

Curiosity and pleasure made her smile, and she looked closely at Milo's sleeping face, trying to gauge how completely he was out. She lifted herself slightly, waiting, but he didn't move. Inching her fingers forward like E.T.'s, and feeling very silly, she reached across his chest and lifted the fortune silently from the dish. She held it close to her face to read:

The journey that matters has no map.

She frowned, turning the paper over, as if there would be another clue on the other side.

"What are you plotting?" Milo asked softly.

She jumped and guiltily put the fortune back in the dish. He had seen, though, and lifted his eyebrows in question.

She smiled. "Is that my fortune?"

"You tell me," he answered.

But she knew. "You saved it," she said, touched by the idea.

"You swallowed mine."

"What do you think it means? The journey of life?"

"You swallowed it and then you kissed me," he continued, as if he hadn't heard her.

She snuggled more closely against him. "I think it means the journey of life."

"I could watch you eat fortunes every day."

She chuckled deep in her throat and set a kiss on his chin.

"Before I became distracted by that slip of paper, I was thinking about your new house," she said.

"So now you'll permit me to move to your town?"

She shifted against him, resting her cheek on his shoulder, and idly fingered a path across his chest. She liked it that he wasn't too hairy. She liked a lot about him, actually.

"Therese?"

"I don't mind," she said.

He groaned. "You could try for a little more enthusiasm."

"I am glad," she repeated. "Does this mean you'll be staying indefinitely?"

When he didn't answer, she shifted her head so that she could look into his face. The humor and pleasure in his gaze had been replaced by the old, steady watchfulness. She could see faint lines of tension around his eyes and wanted to smooth them away. But she waited.

"I need to talk to you about something," he said finally. "Beatrice has invited you for lunch on Saturday. Do you think the restoration will be finished by then?"

"More or less," she said, surprised by his change of subject. "By the following weekend it will certainly be finished. Why?"

"She'll want to take it back to Paris with her."

So this would be the end of the project, she thought. She had known it was coming, but still . . . Her disappointment was like a cold weight in her belly. "Are you leaving too?" she asked.

He tightened his grip on her. "I do have to go. But I want to come back, Therese. Whether I come back or not really depends on you."

Adrenaline began to jump along her nerves. "What do you mean?" she asked.

Milo shifted upward so he could look directly into her eyes. "You've never once reached for me," he said quietly. "Even when we wanted each other so much that it hurt me to stay apart from you, you still held back. It seems like it's a game to you almost. It's not a game to me, Therese. Not an experiment. I can sustain this only so long by myself. You have to want me as much as I want you, or it won't work."

"But I do want you," she objected. She didn't understand his intensity. "Last night was the most amazing experience of my life. You know that, Milo."

He shook his head, entwining her fingers in a tight grip. "I mean on a more fundamental level. I want you in my life forever. I want to know that if I have to go to Paris next week, you'll come with me. Or if you're going to visit your family in Brazil for the holidays, I want to know I can come along too."

She felt a deep, inner hesitation, but he kept going.

"I want a family, Therese," he said, his voice low with emotion. "I want children and a home. I want some child of ours to run through this house, laughing, toppling things over—"

"Stop," she said, her heart twisting at the image of a dark-haired toddler climbing onto Milo's lap. She should feel happy about this, ecstatic, and yet her heart was torn with pained terror. "Do you know what you're saying?"

He continued, undeterred. "I want reality, Therese. And I want it with you."

Her heart was beating rapidly and her chest was tightening, restricting her breath. She pulled her hand free and sat away from him, clutching the sheet to her chest. "You don't know what you're asking," she protested. "It's too soon, Milo! Too soon."

But he didn't seem to hear. His eyes held hers with hypnotic force.

"Reach for me," he said. The simple words resonated between them.

"I can't!"

"Reach for me, darling. Please."

A surge of panic ripped through her. She pushed back along the bed, trying to escape the riveting longing in his eyes, the terrible, heart-wrenching love. Sitting up, he seemed like a tiger that would consume and destroy her, leaving nothing of her peaceful, independent life. He held out his arms to her, and she backed up hard against the footboard of the bed, clutching the covers to her chest. It was like her terror in the studio when the unknown man was lurking outside the door, only this time there was no escape.

She half screamed her resistance. "No!"

For one last, piercing moment, his eyes burned into hers, then a shadow of bewildered pain crossed his face and he looked away. His bare chest was heaving and the muscles of his shoulders were taut. His eyes were hooded and dark, his profile fierce and hard. But he nodded once.

"You don't have to run from me," he said. "It's bad enough you won't reach for me. Get your things. I'll drive you home."

He didn't call her.

She knew why, but it drove her crazy anyway. She

thought he'd call at work, but he didn't. She'd get home, looking for the flashing light on her answering machine, and it would shine as steady and unblinking as a dead cat. Three days passed. Saturday was approaching, the day she was supposed to have lunch with Beatrice, and still he didn't call.

She couldn't go to the studio, even though she'd promised to finish the restoration of Louisa. What if she ran into him? What if he demanded an answer to his ultimatum? What if he kissed her? Or worse, what if he looked like he no longer wanted to?

She didn't know what to do. She didn't know who to call for advice. She couldn't stand the awful gnawing feeling she had in her stomach, or the sleepless edginess that haunted her night and day. If this was love, she thought, it was an awful lot like the flu. It wasn't anything like what she'd felt for Josh, not in a million years. But that didn't bother her anymore. She accepted that what she felt for Milo was different. But was it enough? Was this really love, she wondered, or was it some crazy infatuation worked up by what had happened when they were in bed together?

If only he'd just come back to Brookline, live in his gorgeous house, make love to her regularly, and give them both a chance to get to know each other better. Then she would know. Then she could see if she really loved him.

But deep down she knew that wasn't the answer Milo needed to hear. He had taken a risk earlier when he'd told his story of looking in the rearview mirror at Orrin and his daughter. He had trusted her then, and last night he had taken another risk, an even bigger one, by expecting that she would want to share her life with him.

She was haunted by the flash of confusion and pain she'd seen in his eyes before he turned away from her, that last moment on his bed. He had believed she would be willing to reach for him too. He'd made up his mind. He knew what he wanted. He was decisive and purposeful in all his important decisions. That was why he'd become as successful as he was.

But she was successful too, her inner voice rebelled. And she wouldn't be forced into something unless she was sure.

And with both sides of her mind equally squared off against each other, she stumbled grimly, stubbornly, miserably toward the moment when she would see him again.

Saturday morning, instead of sticking to her plan to avoid the portrait of Louisa, Therese decided to put in a couple more hours of treating the painting before she met Beatrice for lunch. Her stomach felt strange and light as she walked up the last flight of stairs, and she both dreaded and hoped that Milo would be there. So many times they'd been happy together in the studio. Maybe there she would find some resolution for the uncertainty that was eating through her stomach.

She stopped before the door and knocked, then waited, listening. At least Bert or the other guard would be there if Milo wasn't. She heard footsteps, saw the doorknob turn, and she swallowed hard as the door swung inward.

A tall, blond woman with sunglasses propped in her hair was holding the door open.

Therese felt her jaw actually drop.

"Who are you?" she asked. She peered quickly behind the woman and saw Bert in the room.

"I am Veronique de Blanc," the woman said. "Beatrice is my mother. And you must be Mademoiselle Carroll." Veronique smiled politely and opened the door wider to let Therese pass.

Veronique was dressed in a coral-colored sleeveless dress that reminded Therese of Jackie Kennedy. She had gold earrings and gold sandals and the polished air of a wealthy woman beyond her first blush of youth.

Therese's surprise turned to amazement when she saw Milo wasn't also in the studio. "Where is Milo?" she asked Bert.

"At his home, I suppose," Veronique said, answering before Bert could speak.

"Then what are you doing here?" Therese asked.

"I would like to have a word with Milo myself," Veronique said, as if she had misheard. "Why don't we go together?"

Therese moved closer to the painting of Louisa, becoming increasingly suspicious. "I was going to work for a few hours before I meet your mother for lunch. How did you get in here?"

Veronique laughed, smiling at Bert. "Monsieur Bert has been so helpful to me. And his photos of his baby are adorable."

Bert held up his hands in a shrug. "She said her mother sent her," he explained. "She just took a quick look. No harm done."

Therese closed her eyes and mentally groaned. With one good look at Veronique's beautiful face, her poise and assurance, Therese knew instantly that something was very wrong.

"Bert," she said. "Call Milo and tell him what's happened. And tell him I'm coming to see him in person. Now."

Bert's face registered surprise and concern. The last thing Therese wanted to do was get Bert in more trouble with Milo, but his orders were not to let anyone, not *anyone*, in the studio except for her or Milo, and that included conniving beautiful Frenchwomen.

Bert walked quickly to the phone and began to dial.

Therese did an about-face and headed out of the studio.

"But wait!" Veronique called. She caught up with Therese outside, a stylish jacket pulled on over her dress, as Therese was hailing a taxi. "Let me go with you."

"Did you tell Milo you were coming here?" Therese demanded.

"Such hostility!" Veronique said. "Surely there is no cause for such alarm."

Therese planted her hands on her hips as a taxi pulled up in front of her. "That painting's been under twenty-four-hour surveillance ever since it set foot in this country. I nearly got killed because of that painting. Did you tell Milo you were coming or not?"

Veronique's mouth rounded in an O of red lipstick. "But you are charming," she said. "Absolutely perfect. No wonder Milo's been gone from Paris such a long time."

Therese burned with fury and frustration. Clearly she

wasn't going to get a straight answer out of this woman. She wrenched open the taxi door and took her seat, cringing when Veronique slid in beside her.

Therese gave Milo's address to the driver, praying he'd be home. Then she deliberately looked out her window and did her best to ignore Veronique. Resentment and suspicion roiled inside her.

Veronique shifted on the seat, and Therese heard a clicking of beads, jewels. She wore a faint scent too, as if she needed more to prove how intensely feminine she was. How come Therese couldn't remember Milo talking much about Veronique? Was she married? She must be in her midforties, a decade older than Milo. Did that make her sister-type material? Somehow Therese doubted it.

When they reached his house, Milo was waiting on the porch. Therese could see his lean figure as he came down the stairs, and her heart twisted at the stern expression on his face. He wore a suit similar to the one he'd worn when she first met him. She sensed instinctively that the last three days had done something to him, honed him somehow. He opened their door and paid the driver while Therese and Veronique got out of the taxi.

"I have met your restoration expert, Milo," Veronique said. "What a shame I never met her father. Is there much of a resemblance?"

Milo gave Veronique an unreadable stare, then ushered her toward the house.

"Bert called me," he said to Therese. "This doesn't surprise me."

He opened the front door and Therese followed Veronique inside. She felt an instant of hesitation, remembering the last time she'd been there, when Milo had made love to her and urged her to reach for him. She felt the color begin to rise along her neck, but Veronique provided a distraction, warmly admiring the house and everything in it. When Therese glanced at Milo, he seemed reserved, his response to Veronique measured and civil.

"Ah! The teapots!" Veronique exclaimed as they entered the library. "Highlights of your collection. Isn't there a story about teapots and the Boston Harbor?"

Milo's stern expression seemed to melt slightly as he glanced at Therese. "Something like that," he said.

Therese couldn't help a smile.

Veronique stepped close to the mantel, then brought her sunglasses out of her hair and down to her eyes, peering through them to inspect one of the teapots before she realized her mistake.

"Oh!" she exclaimed. "One never has the right glasses when one needs them." She tucked them in her purse.

"I hope you had the right ones at the studio," Milo said.

"It has been so fascinating to hear all about Mama's painting," Veronique said. "I knew we would be talking about it over lunch, and I just had to take a quick look, you know, so I could follow along."

Therese was getting used to the way Veronique never answered a question. It was a little like watching a trick with mirrors.

"I hope you were satisfied," Milo said.

Veronique smiled and put a hand on her hip, accentuating the smallness of her waist. "Indeed. The work on Louisa is exquisite. If only the rest of us could get such face-lifts."

Milo shook his head, reluctantly amused. Therese relaxed too, letting her guard down for the first time since she'd met Veronique.

"There's only one question I have." Veronique pursed her lips. "What about the ring? When do you intend to tell poor Mama you have found her emeralds?"

Therese could have dropped a knife through the silence. Her gaze flew to Milo's face, to the cold mask that had quickly covered his features. It was impossible that he hadn't told Beatrice about the emeralds yet! That was the whole point of the restoration.

"Milo?" she asked, astonished.

His eyebrows lowered and his expression darkened dangerously, but he didn't answer Therese. Clearly observing the two of them, Veronique laughed.

"Oh, but there is misunderstanding here! I am so clumsy."

"Not clumsy," Milo said. "As deft as ever. What else do you have to say, Veronique? Let's hear it."

She opened her hands in exaggerated innocence. "Only that Mama will be so happy to know. It is hard to keep such news from someone who is losing her eyesight so rapidly. You can't mean to delay much longer, for all you have very good reasons, I'm sure."

"Very good," Milo said. He folded his arms across his chest.

"I'm sure Mother will be glad to hear them. You always have such a way of bringing her around, after all. And she trusts you so, more than a son in so many ways."

Therese saw a faint hint of color under Milo's tanned complexion and knew Veronique had hit a sensitive nerve. She was bewildered, though, and amazed. Why hadn't

Milo told Beatrice about the painting? It didn't make sense.

"I'm sure you have other things to do before we meet her for lunch," Milo said.

"Oh, yes!" Veronique said. "And now that I have seen your enchanting home, I will be able to tell her all about it too. It reminds me a little of that place you bought in Nice. But you only owned that for six months, didn't you?" She began to walk out of the library toward the front door.

"This isn't *anything* like the place in Nice," Milo said. Then, "Wait here," he said quietly to Therese.

She could hear him following Veronique through the house, the woman's voice light and melodic, his answers barely audible rumbles. Therese felt the floor tipping under her as she tried to make sense out of the exchange she had just witnessed. Milo seemed like another person when he was with Veronique, cynical and dry, defensive and wary. And Veronique!

Whew, Therese thought. She'd never met anyone like Veronique.

When Milo returned to the library and walked slowly over to the desk, Therese was forcibly reminded of the first time she'd met him in A.K.'s office. In many ways that seemed like a million years before, yet his face belonged to that stranger, poised and masterful, yet cool, infinitely reserved. She shivered, and he glanced over at her. His frown intensified.

"You haven't told Beatrice about the ring," she said quietly. She hoped he would deny it, even now.

He ran his hand through his dark hair, then rubbed

the back of his neck. "I was going to tell her today, at lunch, with you there."

"But the whole point of the restoration was to find her emeralds," Therese said, keeping her voice calm. "You were in such a hurry about it. Why didn't you tell her?"

His eyes skimmed away from hers.

"The timing was wrong," he said. "It was too soon after that crazy night with the false security guard at the studio, and she was angry. If I'd told her then, she would have taken the next flight back to France to confront her cousin Thomas."

She didn't believe him. "Who is she? A child who can't be trusted with her own judgment?"

"It would have been a mistake to tell her."

Therese didn't like it. "It was her prerogative to go or stay," she said. "And you didn't tell me. You let me believe you'd told her about the ring."

Once again he'd proven he was an expert of omission. Milo didn't need to lie; he could deceive with a clear conscience.

"I couldn't tell her," he said. "She would have taken the picture, and I would have had to go with her. What would you have thought if I'd left that next day?"

Therese bit her lip and lowered her head, trying to remember. They had made love that night in the studio. Their relationship had just turned a corner, and if he'd really left then, it was true she would have been hurt and confused.

But she had believed she could trust him, and now she wasn't so sure. She looked back up at him, searching his face.

"Try to understand," he said. "Beatrice trusts me to do this the right way, as she trusted me to find the painting and the right person to restore it. She won't question my timing when she discovers I waited a few days to tell her about the emerald ring. But there's something about the painting I still don't understand, Therese, some elusive detail I can't figure out. I genuinely don't know why your father didn't bring the painting back to her, and this troubles me. I feel like it's the key to the whole problem."

"That was fifteen years ago! You have an elderly, almost blind woman depending utterly on your judgment. Where are your loyalties?"

Milo went completely still, his face draining of color.

"You sound like Veronique," he said quietly. "Only she wasn't so blunt."

Therese felt a knife twist in her chest. "She seems to know you well."

He gave a cold laugh. "She tolerates me. She resents me. She thinks her mother cares more for me than she does for her, which is absurd."

Now Therese had a better understanding of Veronique's comment when she'd said Milo could bring Beatrice around and that Beatrice had always trusted him. It could be that Veronique was jealous of him, but she'd also dropped that barbed comment about Milo's house in Nice. It stung to think he'd brought property before on the chance he'd impress a woman.

He was watching her closely, and she angled her face away, hoping he couldn't read her thoughts.

"What is it?" he asked. "What else is the problem?"

She licked her lips and swallowed hard. "Do you often buy houses for such a short time?"

His eyes narrowed, then he laughed and turned away from her, walking toward the window. "I bought that so my soccer friends and I would have a place to vacation one winter. Then one of my friends bought me out. It was nothing like this situation here in Brookline, despite what Veronique implied. But if you're looking for reasons to doubt me, Therese, you can find hundreds."

She knotted her hands together and tried to quiet the agitation she felt. "I don't *want* to doubt you," she said, then winced. It was obvious that she doubted him enormously.

He turned back to face her, and she could see the hurt behind his cold expression. She thought for an instant that he would throw something, lash out at her, but he merely laughed again, a bitter, self-recriminatory laugh that sounded too raw to her.

"You're wise to doubt me," he said. "Wisdom goes well with integrity, and you've always had that."

She flinched as if he'd hit her. He wasn't being fair. Only three nights before, in this very room, they'd initiated the intimacy that had changed her life and set her whole world spinning in another direction. Now she didn't know what the truth was, but she certainly wasn't going to learn it from him, bitter and sarcastic as he was being.

Slowly she walked toward the door, proudly squaring her shoulders.

"Please tell Beatrice I can't make it to lunch," she said.

"What?"

"I'm going to the studio." She looked him straight in

the eye, without apology, without artifice. "I need to finish my obligation to restore Louisa as soon as possible."

"That won't solve what's between us," he argued.

"We've found we can hurt each other. And though you don't lie, technically, your omissions are just as deceptive. This is probably a good place to stop."

"It's not that simple, Therese."

Reaching behind her, she gripped the cool glass doorknob, bracing the edge of the door against her back.

He walked toward her. "Don't leave like this."

She felt her body instantly tighten with awareness at his approach, as if she were full of magnetic filings and he were the North Pole. If he touched her, she didn't know what she was going to do.

"It doesn't help to stay," she said. "I only get more confused when I'm around you."

He was even nearer, standing only an arm's length before her. She tightened her grip on the doorknob. It was his eyes that were troubling her the most. His dark, watchful eyes could read her secrets somehow, understand and dismiss her confusion as surface tension, while he identified the deeper truths beneath.

"Are you more confused now?" he asked.

Her heart charged against her ribs. She nodded.

He reached out and slid his warm hands up her arms to her elbows, drawing her to him. "And now?" he asked.

She was more confused, and yet, at the same time, heat was stealing through her, pushing logical thought to the side. He brought his body even closer until her chest touched his, and she had to let go of the doorknob and steady herself against him. She looked up at him helplessly.

"Damn," he muttered, and kissed her.

She closed her eyes and half swooned against him, knowing this was where she'd been longing to be, even if this was their last kiss ever. His arms crushed her, his kiss deepened, and she felt the velvet depths of her respond with undeniable hunger. Her body remembered their intimacy, and she molded her body to his, feeling the quick heat between them as if their clothes were as thin as silk.

He released her suddenly and backed up a pace, visibly shaken. She saw him drag a hand through his hair and his eyes flashed with a hint of anger.

"You can't help responding," he said. "Doesn't that mean anything to you?"

"Of course it does."

She was tingling and frustrated from being released so abruptly. Her whole body ached to be against his. She bit inward on her sensitive lips and tried to calm the erratic beating of her heart. Now that he'd allowed some space between them, her confusion was back tenfold.

She didn't like being confused, she thought. "If you wouldn't try to hurry me, maybe I could figure out what it means," she said irritably.

But she could see this only evoked answering irritation in him.

"What have you been thinking about the last three days?" he demanded.

You, she thought. But she didn't speak. She reached to the back of her neck for her braid and pulled it forward, sliding her hand down it to the end. She could see his eyes following the movement with steady concentration, as if even this simple gesture was something that fascinated him. And he was still waiting for an answer.

"Well?" he said.

"I've been thinking about reality."

His eyes flashed to hers. "And how I fit into it?" he asked.

She didn't know the answer to that yet. He looked half starved and savage at the same time, as if he'd wring the answer out of her if he could. It wasn't so much that he frightened her, she realized. It was the matching intensity of her own emotions that startled and alarmed her. Could she afford to care this much about someone? Someone she hardly knew? Was it enough to trust on instinct when her logic told her otherwise?

She studied his handsome face, the dark eyebrows and brooding gray eyes. She imprinted on her mind the contours of his jaw and cheekbones, the half-tamed texture of his dark hair, as if these physical characteristics would summon the answer she needed. But she didn't know, and she couldn't pretend she did.

"Tell Beatrice about the ring," she said, then turned to let herself out.

NINE

Therese took a taxi back to the studio and climbed the stairs two at a time, trying to burn off the energy of her anger. She hated being confused. She hated being pushed. She hated wanting to kiss him when she knew she couldn't do it. He was using her own body against her, playing her like a finely tuned harp. And she didn't like it.

"You're back," Bert said, as he let her in. "Everything all right? Aren't you supposed to be having lunch?"

"Everything's terrific," she said.

Bert reacted as if she were a hungry lion, tiptoeing back to his chair and hiding behind his latest roll of baby pictures.

Therese whipped off her coat, marched over to the portrait, and stared down at Louisa. The sweet face of the young girl was as serene as ever, but Therese felt mocked by the composure she saw there. Gone was her sense of triumph at finding the ring. Instead she felt only the too familiar anger and confusion. Milo should have told Beatrice about the ring right away, no matter what.

Except that he might have had to leave for Paris immediately. And he hadn't wanted to go.

So did that mean he was putting his relationship with her before his obligations to Beatrice? It couldn't be possible.

Or did he still, somehow, think he could use Therese's memories to reveal why her father hadn't wanted to give the painting back to Beatrice?

Every instinct revolted against the last idea, but Therese remained resentful and unsure.

She picked up her brush and tried to start the inpainting work she'd abandoned five nights before, but for the first time in her life she couldn't concentrate on her work. She squinted over a patch of paint and nearly cried in frustration.

What was wrong with her?

She groaned softly, pushing a tendril of black hair out of her eyes.

It couldn't be that she was in love with him! Love wasn't supposed to be like this. Love was supposed to be an expansive, happy feeling, with heady bouquets of flowers and a devoted, sweet-talking man.

Instead she had Milo, a fierce, obsessive person who wanted to take over her reality with zero advance notice. When she tried to slow down, he sped up. When she spoke of wisdom and integrity, he transformed the honorable words into wounding accusations. When she argued they needed more time to know each other, he became frustrated because he thought she didn't trust him.

But how could she trust him? Beatrice trusted him, and he hadn't even told her about the ring.

And then he'd used his body to short-circuit her logic.

Therese closed her eyes and tried to clear her mind, but it was hopeless. So if she didn't know him enough, and she didn't trust him, and she was terrified about him leaving or staying, and she didn't love him, then why couldn't she think of anything but him?

Therese didn't know how much later it was when she heard a noise at the door. She looked up, blinking out of her fog, just as the doorknob turned and Milo opened the door.

For a fleeting, heart-soaring moment she was glad to see him, but when she registered the sober expression on his face, her heart plummeted and her anxiety returned.

Milo stepped back to let an elderly woman precede him into the studio, then turned to quietly close the door. Therese concealed her surprise with a professional, welcoming smile.

"I'd like you to meet Therese Carroll," Milo said to the woman next to him. "Beatrice de Blanc."

Beatrice stepped ahead of him, a smile gracing her calm, lined face. She was a diminutive woman, even dainty, with a modest green coat and stylish ankle boots. Therese looked for a resemblance to Veronique and found it in the firmness of the jaw, the proud carriage. But age had eased something in the small woman, softened her edges. Therese looked again and was caught by Beatrice's eyes: the paleness of her blue irises, the odd dilation of her pupils. Her large blue-rimmed glasses were jaunty and youthful, but the lenses were thick. Beatrice could still see, that was certain, but she seemed to look around her for shapes, not for minute details. Therese felt an inner softening of sympathy for her.

"*Bonjour, mademoiselle,*" Beatrice said.

"Beatrice understands English," Milo explained, "but she doesn't speak it well."

"How do you do?" Therese said. She started to come forward to shake hands, but Beatrice waved her back to her work area.

"She'd like you to show her what you're doing," Milo said to Therese.

At last, Therese thought. She stepped back to the portrait, placing Beatrice with the best view, and explained her work with precise gestures. She told Beatrice how she'd treated the painting, from the ultraviolet light inspection to when she'd undermined the overpaint on Louisa's hand. She couldn't keep the pride from her voice as she showed how the colors came through clearly now, how the painting, as a whole, was nearly as subtle and rich as it had been when it was first completed, nearly two hundred years before.

"Here," she said, pointing to a strip in the lower right-hand corner and at a section of Louisa's hair. "After the removal of the natural resin varnish, you can see these last bits needed to be retouched. It will only take a few more days, then I'll apply another protective varnish."

When Beatrice was silent, Therese glanced up to Milo to see if the woman had understood and he nodded. She looked for any other sign from him, any personal recognition of what had passed between them, but his face was a mask of indifferent civility. Aching inside, she returned her attention to Beatrice. The old woman stood before the painting, her gaze roving over it. Therese had handed her the magnifying glass, but the woman didn't bother holding it up. She merely looked, finally shaking her head in amazement.

"*Magnifique,*" she said. "*Elle devait etre si plein des ombres. Et maintenant—seulement la lumière.*"

Milo smiled at Beatrice, then spoke to Therese. "You've taken away the shadows and given her light," he translated. Then he raised his hand and touched his shirt pocket.

His heart, she thought. So he wasn't completely indifferent to her after all, despite how he was acting in front of Beatrice. A fragile feeling started in her gut, but she was afraid to look up and meet his gaze.

Beatrice began speaking in French to Milo, and her voice was now clipped and businesslike. Milo gave her his full attention, and Therese watched him slip his hands into his pockets, frowning gravely.

She waited for the translation, growing nervous.

When Milo turned to her, his neutral expression baffled her. He cleared his throat.

"Beatrice wants to know if you've looked beneath the pearl necklace."

"Beneath the original paint of the pearl?" she asked, confused. "There was no need to. The fluorescence under the UV light was perfect in that area. You remember. And it cleaned up beautifully once the soot and varnish were removed, like the paint of the skin tones on her chest around it. See here," she said, pointing to the smoothness of the paint.

Beatrice shook her head, then spoke to Milo.

Therese had never seen his face go so motionless before, as if he had slid a stone mask over every feature. The result was unnerving, as if he were still Milo but someone else too.

"She wants you to test beneath the pearl," he said, "the way you tested beneath the clover-shaped patch on the finger."

She couldn't believe what he was saying.

"That patch on her hand was different," she said. "It was black under the UV, like the other places that had been overpainted. The pearl is original, I'm certain."

Milo began translating for Beatrice, but the older woman cut him off.

"I understand her," she said, then went on in French, directing herself to Milo.

His face remained carefully unresponsive, as if he'd steeled himself to withstand a painfully uncomfortable ordeal, and Therese became increasingly alarmed.

"Excuse us a moment," he said to Therese, and guided Beatrice over to one of the windows.

In hushed tones Milo and Beatrice continued their conversation in rapid French. There was nothing mellow about the older woman now. She bore herself with regal composure, but her voice was laced with steel. Milo was respectful but insistent. Beatrice responded with even icier commands.

Therese glanced over at Bert, whose eyes were wide. He blinked at her, then grimaced. Looks bad, he seemed to be saying.

No kidding, Therese thought. All she could do was wait and be concerned.

There was a pause, then the older woman spoke clearly. *"Ton amie est charmante, Milo. La vraie fille de*

Harry. Mais vraiment. Nous parlons des émeraudes ici. Des émeraudes, oui?"

Beatrice patted Milo on the arm, and it didn't take a translator to see the condescension in the gesture. Therese didn't know what Beatrice had said, but Milo's composure finally shifted and a ruddy flush rose under his tan. For a moment his eyes focused on Beatrice, then he pursed his lips in a French fashion and turned to stare out the window.

Therese felt a stone roll over in her belly. He's lost, she thought. What did this mean for them?

Beatrice turned to her again, smiling as graciously as before. Therese shivered, seeing now that Beatrice's practiced smile was as false as the finest cosmetic mud.

"Thank you, my dear," she said to Therese. She kissed her fingertips and gestured with them toward the painting, as if it were a delicious morsel of cake.

"Of course," Therese answered.

"I'll just see her down to the cab," Milo said, his voice strained. In another moment they left the studio and headed down the stairs. Bert closed the door carefully behind them.

"Whew," he said, turning back to Therese.

She felt exactly the same way. She sagged against her stool, gingerly wiping her forehead.

"She's a regular pterodactyl," Bert said.

"It's going to get worse," she predicted.

"Milo? He's not such a stick. He'll take her orders with a grain of salt."

"I don't know." She couldn't get over the way he'd finally blushed and turned to look out the window.

And when, several minutes later, he came back up, she

knew instantly they were in for trouble. His expression was hardened like granite; his eyes were molten with cold fury. Bert took one look at him, whistled a low note, grabbed his coat, and fled.

Milo slowly slipped his white scarf from around his neck, keeping his gaze directed at the floor, so she had the feeling he was avoiding her, stalling for time. She could feel the tension emanating from him.

"I hope Beatrice wasn't too upset that I missed lunch," she said lightly.

He didn't smile. He pulled the length of cashmere through his long fingers, and she saw a muscle in his jaw clench.

"All right," she said. "I could see it was bad. Just get it over with." They were going to take the picture, unfinished, back to France.

"You must look under the pearl," he said.

It was so unexpected, so ridiculous, she had to laugh with relief.

"But, Milo, that's preposterous," she said. "You remember that first day when we took the painting into the closet, with the UV light."

"How could I forget?"

She felt a warmth rising in her cheeks. "The area on Louisa's body was evenly green, remember? It was one of the areas that had no damage at all, aside from the soot discoloration. You can see now there are even places where the oil paint bled the slightest bit into the flesh color, which could only happen if the paint was still slightly wet when the necklace was painted on. It's a sure sign of original work. I'll show you," she repeated, urging him toward the painting.

He remained stubbornly beside the desk.

"You don't understand," he said. "You must look beneath it anyway. Beatrice wants to be absolutely certain Thomas's other emeralds aren't hidden beneath."

"What other emeralds?"

"The ones in the ring and necklace set that Thomas gave his wife. Remember?"

She shook her head. "But they're completely irrelevant. There's nothing underneath," she insisted. "Just gesso and the canvas itself. Exploring beneath the original paint of the pearl would only ruin it. It would ruin the entire painting."

She felt a jolt as she again remembered her father's rhyme. Here was the searching greed that would destroy even the empty oyster, only now she was supposed to destroy the painted pearl.

"We can't do it, Milo!" she said urgently. "It would ruin Louisa! That's what my father was afraid of, all those years ago. I'm certain of it."

But Milo hardly seemed to be listening. "You could patch it up again afterward if you want to," he said.

" 'If I want to'! 'Patch it up'!" she echoed, astounded. For a moment she was absolutely speechless. "This is my life's work, Milo, and I guarantee you there's nothing beneath the pearl. I'd stake my whole reputation on it." She waved an irate hand. "Look under the pearl! I might just as easily look under the background to see if there's anything hanging from her bare earlobe."

Milo sent his eyes toward the ceiling. "Don't let Beatrice hear you say that."

"Well, Milo, really." Therese let out a laugh. "Explain to her what I've said. She'll understand. If her eyesight weren't so bad I could convince her myself."

He shook his head and with a tired gesture stuffed his scarf into the pocket of his overcoat. "The blindness here has nothing to do with Beatrice's eyes."

Therese folded her arms across her chest. "That makes it even worse."

"No, it doesn't," he said. "It only makes my obligation to her all the stronger." His jaw hardened, as if he had to remind himself of it. "I've already made one mistake by not telling her instantly when you found the ring. You were right about that. Now, whether I agree with her or not, I owe it to her to follow through on her wishes. It's her painting, after all, to cherish or destroy as she sees fit."

Therese straightened proudly to her full height. "I won't do it."

She saw Milo's hands clench into fists.

"Then I'll just have to find someone else who will."

The shock of his words made her go utterly still. Then the pain sliced through her. She turned her back on him and paced quickly over to the windows. Never before had she felt so hurt, so wounded. The insult went far deeper than a professional slur. She felt the blow to her very core, as if he didn't trust her. As if he questioned her integrity.

How could he let the painting be ruined, just for Beatrice's greedy curiosity? She summoned her strength and turned to face him.

"Think back," she said, striving to keep her voice reasonable. "Remember when we first uncrated the portrait together? Your face looked like you'd seen heaven, Milo. The painting has a unique power of its own." She lifted one hand, imploring. "Who is to say the emeralds of Beatrice's dream, no matter how priceless they are, are worth more than this painting just as it stands? Even if we knew there were emeralds beneath the pearl, would it be worth it to discover them at the cost of this beauty?"

She stepped quickly to the worktable and tilted the painting so that he could see it upright, as if it were hanging on a wall. She stood beside it, willing him to see Louisa as he had first seen her, with all his hope and longing. He had understood the innocence then; it had touched some core of him, stolen his jaded heart and given it back to him larger, more generous than before. If he could just see that magic again, he couldn't ask her to destroy the painting.

But when he finally looked over, he hardly glanced at the picture. Instead his gaze lingered on her own face, until Therese could feel it like a feather of heat that trailed across her forehead and down the bridge of her nose and across her lips. She licked the sudden dryness she felt there and saw a flicker of response in his eyes.

He came nearer and reached for the portrait, relieving her of its weight. Gently he laid it back on the table.

Bracing his hands on the table, he leaned his head down as if the weight of what he was thinking was a stone around his neck.

"You are making this nearly impossible for me," he said at last.

She backed up a step.

"Don't look so betrayed," he begged her. "Try to see this from another angle for a second. Is there any chance your feelings for the picture have prevented you from seeing the pearl might not be original? Are you possibly being prejudiced by your father's actions?"

"No. Absolutely not."

He tried another tack. "Have you never disagreed with another art conservator on how something ought to be restored?"

She hesitated, leaning back against the counter of the kitchenette and crossing her arms. "I've disagreed a few times," she admitted. "In almost every case I ended up being right."

"So experts do sometimes disagree."

"Yes. But the more expertise they have, the more likely they are to agree on how to treat a painting. And, Milo, bragging aside, I really am very good at what I do. Ask Mickey. I'm not wrong about Louisa's pearl."

"Ask Mickey," he repeated, jumping on her suggestion. "So you agree a second opinion would only strengthen your assessment?"

She frowned, distrustful of where this was going. But she was confident she was right. Any of her colleagues who examined Louisa would back her up.

"It would confirm my assessment," she said.

Milo let out a big breath and smiled. "Then we have nothing to worry about."

Her heart went cold. "What do you mean?"

"I mean I'm taking the picture back to Paris for Beatrice. Where we can find another restorer."

So she had been right. He was taking the painting away from her. She couldn't even finish her job, let alone protect Louisa from real damage. He would take the painting to some hack restorer who wasn't even program-trained and let him dig under the pearl.

"If you had any integrity at all, you'd tell Beatrice you won't do it," she said.

He came around the table toward her, but she backed away. He stopped where he was, frowning.

"There's more than one kind of integrity," he said, his voice low. "I understand you're defending art. But there are some values even above art, Therese." His gaze was serious and unwavering. "The painting belongs to Beatrice. Even if she's unreasonable, she's relying on me to uphold her rights. There's another form of integrity that comes from doing what you know is right, even if you have to sacrifice art to do it."

She refused to believe the painting should be ruined. "Then do what's right, Milo, and persuade Beatrice not to destroy the painting."

He ran his hand rapidly through his hair, as if exasperated with himself that he couldn't convince her. "Please understand," he said. "I can't do that. Beatrice knows nothing of your kind of work. When dealing with something this precious and with the potential for priceless emeralds, it's common prudence to ask two experts, and she knows this."

"What about all the secrecy?" she asked, grasping at anything.

"You've already found the ring," he pointed out. "Beatrice and Veronique have both seen it. Thomas wouldn't dare damage or steal the painting now. It would only point more suspicion at him."

She put a hand on her hip and pressed her lips together.

"Be careful," she said. Her voice became cool as anger moved in to cover her hurt. "There's a difference between a trained conservator and a restorer. If you find a hack who can do the work on short notice, you'll be dealing with someone who can be bought, someone who might butcher that pearl for an easy fee."

He tilted his head, watching her closely. "Unlike you."

His voice was soft, but she thought she heard sarcasm in his words. A bitter laugh escaped her. "You never bought me, Milo. You charmed me and seduced me, but you never bought me. I've done this for my father."

"You misunderstand me," he said.

She turned from him, staring blindly out the window at the late afternoon light that touched the new leaves on the trees. They shimmered through her unshed tears, and she blinked hard.

"You've used me, Milo," she said. "You let me exhaust myself doing a meticulous job on this portrait when all along you really only wanted me to locate the emeralds. I could have used a garden trowel for all you cared. Now you don't even have the grace to let me complete my work. In case you didn't know, that is the basest of professional insults. Add to it the way you . . ." She couldn't begin to describe what he'd done to her personally.

He crossed the room swiftly and stood inches from her, blocking her view of the bright windows.

"I never deceived you about this, Therese. Look at me."

She blinked hard, then lifted her gaze. She was impressed by the remorse in his piercing eyes, the seeming sincerity, but she could no longer be deceived. Though her body ached to close the distance between them, to launch herself into his arms, she stood proudly, waiting to see how far he'd go to convict himself.

"I'm not asking you to look under the pearl anymore," he said, "because I accept that you can't. I'm asking for something bigger now. I want you to look beyond the painting, and beyond Beatrice." His voice dropped to a hush that gripped her with its honesty. "You have to look beyond all the work you've put into this project, and beyond what your father would have thought in a situation like this. I want you to look in your heart, Therese, and see if you trust me to do the right thing."

Therese felt a stone twist and fall deep inside her. She felt as if he were taking away her strength when she needed it most, and this seemed like the worst manipulation of all. She wanted to trust him, but to trust him meant the painting might be destroyed, and that would be like destroying a part of herself.

She shook her head, unable to speak.

He came one step nearer and waited until she again raised her eyes to his. "We can't always agree," he said. "But we have to trust each other, Therese." His eyes seemed to consume her. "I love you more than I ever believed I could love anyone."

For a long, agonizing moment his words hung between them. She couldn't believe how much it hurt her to hear them, because she was certain he was lying. Even if he believed he was speaking the truth, his actions proved he'd never loved her.

"I don't know why it still matters to you to insist on this charade," she said quietly. "I think even the most egotistical man would give it up at the end."

She saw him flinch but felt no satisfaction in knowing she'd hurt him too.

She turned away from him, gliding quickly across the studio to the door. Her gaze touched on the bed, his desk, the computer and the kitchenette, the sunny rectangles of the windows, and finally the portrait of Louisa. She knew she'd always want to remember this space, this last moment with Milo, no matter how painful it was. But she didn't look back to see the tortured face of the man who'd said he loved her, the man who watched helplessly as she pulled the door closed.

TEN

For three weeks Therese woke up every morning and buried her head under the pillow. It took three attacks on the snooze button before her alarm clock could convince her to get out of bed and then she shuffled disconsolately around her apartment, feeling lost in her own space, wishing she didn't have to clean up and get to work. Mickey gave her a raise, more vacation time, extra space at the lab, but she couldn't have cared less. All she could think about was Milo Dansforth, Total Heartbreaker. It gnawed at her all day. Then at night, when she tried to sleep, her heart twisted inward on itself, betrayed her, and she missed Milo with a longing that made it hard for her to breathe.

She kept hearing the soft hush of his voice when he'd told her he loved her, only now the cruel mockery of it left her nerves raw. If his words were even partly true, he would have called by now, but day after day ticked by and she heard nothing from him. He didn't even send a check to pay her. She'd never even been reimbursed for those ridiculous groceries she'd bought for him that first day at the studio. He had vanished, their relationship as incomplete as the restoration of Louisa had been.

One evening she walked up to the door of her apartment building carrying a load of groceries, knowing she had no appetite. It was April now, with spring full-fledged and bursting around her, but instead of savoring the voices of the happy children in the city parks, she kept her eyes on the squares of concrete before her, finding tiny eddies of winter sand where it had been washed up by the rain.

She opened her mailbox and took out a postcard from an aunt in São Paulo, then propped it against the toaster when she got upstairs.

There was one small comfort in all of this. She knew her father again in another way. He must have known that Beatrice had wanted her emeralds and that she would dig beneath the pearl if she ever recovered the painting. Seeing the purity and beauty captured in the portrait of the child bride, her father had preferred to leave Louisa behind in Romania rather than deliver her up to Beatrice's greed. In her own way Therese had made the same choice her father had, but even this made her uneasy rather than proud.

She unloaded her groceries and thought pessimistically that her father had only delayed the inevitable. Even now Louisa was probably smiling over a hole in her chest. She tossed a frozen entrée on the counter with a discouraging *plop*, and little flakes of ice began to melt off it.

She closed her eyes, remembering the winter picnic she'd had with Milo, the elusive charm and romance of that first intimate evening in the solarium.

"Oh, Milo!" she whispered.

She hurried into her living room and curled into a corner of her double rocker. With the toe of one foot, she rocked herself, trying to find comfort in the rhythmic movement and the familiar paintings and photographs that surrounded her, but her loneliness was too deep. She thought of the first time she'd met him in the studio; how surprised she'd been by his sleepy eyes when he opened the door. She thought of the night they'd worked together, when she'd studied his reflection in the window, feeling like a fascinated spy until he turned to look at her. Then there was the night when she'd been frightened by the false security guard and Milo had burst into the studio looking ready to wrestle with the police. She smiled sadly. And later that night, when he'd made love to her. Her bones melted again and she hugged her arms around her.

"It's no use," she whispered. But the memories kept coming anyway: the dinner with the cheesecake dessert, the sunny walk in the park across from the museum, the teapots in his library. Was he buying the house still? She had been afraid to drive by in case there was a For Sale sign in the yard.

She stood and impulsively walked over to the watercolor painting of the girl in the garden. She lifted it carefully from its hook and turned it over, tracing her finger lightly over the inscription from her father. "I love my darling Therese more than three full moons. Happy Birthday."

But he was gone, she thought. And now she'd lost Milo too. She sat down on the rocker again, peering far out the windows toward the horizon. What if Milo was right about her father after all? Could her father's love of art have been too extreme? Therese had always loved him for it, but had his passion actually caused him to make the wrong decisions?

She thought back to Milo's story of the night in the basement, when her father had been torn between saving the paintings and escaping to safety himself. Perhaps if he had abandoned the paintings when he and Milo first knew the police were coming, both he and Milo could have escaped and Milo wouldn't have had to spend three years in prison. Awful possibility. She would never know.

But what about Beatrice? Her father had deliberately lost Beatrice's painting again, even though it had rightfully belonged to her. He must have known that Beatrice would ruin the painting for the sake of her emeralds, and once he'd fallen under Louisa's spell, he must have changed his mind about returning it to Beatrice. Was that fair or right? She had never doubted this before, but now she was troubled.

And what about herself? she wondered. She had let herself become so engrossed with Louisa that the painting had mattered more to her than her relationship with Milo. She felt a shiver of dread. Was she so like her father that she would place art above everything, even above love?

Therese gazed longingly at the watercolor of the girl in the garden, remembering all the times she had wished she were in it. But she wasn't a child, she thought. And life wasn't a pretty painting.

Milo had been right about one thing. They needed to trust each other. No matter how much she'd been insulted professionally, no matter how betrayed she'd felt, she could have forgiven him and gone on with him if she'd truly loved him. That was what he'd been saying, although she'd been too angry to fully understand.

She could almost hear his voice arguing with her, pleading with her.

And yet he didn't call.

He was waiting for her to reach for him first, she realized with a start. It was his crazy ultimatum still. Even now, especially now, he wouldn't be satisfied unless she reached for him first.

It actually made her laugh.

That had to be it. But how could she reach for him if he wasn't even in Brookline anymore? She felt her mind go very still and her fingers become cold. Could she go to Paris? She closed her eyes, trying to see if she had the courage. She knew where Gallerie Alvina was on the rue du Bac and she might find him at work there. What if she got all the way there and he didn't love her any longer?

She opened her eyes and gazed determinedly out the windows to where the sun was hovering on the horizon. Maybe she was insane, she thought. But she had to find out if there was any chance for them. With a couple of phone calls, she was booked on the first flight out on Saturday morning, four days ahead.

Therese was working in the museum lab the next day, treating a small section of the German triptych in an effort to get her work finished before she left for Paris on Saturday, when her assistant asked if she wanted to take a call.

"It's a woman," Kate said, her eyes sympathetic, as if she knew it wasn't the voice Therese wanted to hear.

Therese reached for her extension. "Hello?" she said.

A faint crackle gave away that it was long distance. "Allo? Mademoiselle Carroll?"

Therese jumped. "Yes?"

"Beatrice de Blanc here. I hope I not disturb."

"Not at all," Therese said, her heart pounding.

She swiveled her chair so that her amazement would be hidden from the others in the lab. *Stay calm*, she told herself. This was probably just about the restoration bill. Milo wouldn't be behind this.

"It is awkward," Beatrice said in her broken English. "This pearl, you know. How do I say? She was wrong. She was mistake."

Therese gripped the receiver tightly. "You mean you looked beneath the pearl? And there was nothing there?"

"Exactement," Beatrice said, clearly satisfied she'd been understood.

Therese smiled sadly. "Well, thank you for letting me know," she said. "And I'm glad that at least you have your ring. Did Thomas give it back to you yet?"

"Thomas. Yes. He keeps the ring. He give it to his wife, you see. I not want it back now."

Therese laughed, the first mirth she'd felt in weeks. "You just wanted to know, didn't you? It must be an enormous relief to you. I hope you and your cousin are friends again."

Beatrice's laugh came over the line. "After so much years of resentment, it is strange to be smiles," she said. "But this is not why I call. It is Louisa."

An odd sense of expectation trailed along the back of Therese's neck. "Yes?"

"You must fix."

Her throat went dry. "You want me to repair the portrait? Fix the pearl that was damaged by your new conservator?"

"Milo said you were *intelligente*. This is my wish exactly."

Therese froze at the mention of Milo's name. "Is this Milo's idea?" she asked.

"*Mais non!* He would take the knife to me if he know I call. So proud, this man. But I must beg you to restore the painting. I will pay to have you work, very much, no matter. You can come to Paris to do it?" Beatrice's voice lifted high with her request.

A strange longing registered in Therese's heart when she heard of Milo's pride. That was just how he would act, she realized. She looked down at her fingers, gripping them into a fist. It seemed ironic that Beatrice was asking her to go to Paris, just when she'd made plans to visit. But she couldn't work there.

"I tell you what," she said. "You send the portrait here to me at the museum and I'll work on it when I can. I'm very interested in the picture for its own sake, and it will be a relief to me to get it properly finished."

"This is good!" Beatrice said. "I am satisfied with this plan."

At least somebody was, Therese thought. She was definitely unnerved by the idea of having Louisa back in her life. But it was a peace offering from Beatrice, and she had to accept it. She licked her lips, longing to ask about Milo.

"You are doing well?" Beatrice asked.

Therese smiled. "Very well, thank you. I hope your eyesight is doing as well as possible."

"As expected," Beatrice replied. "I am learning Braille now, for later on. Veronique interviews the dogs."

Therese nodded. She knew it must be a sad and frightening experience. A new rush of sympathy for the older woman made her glad she'd agreed to finish the restoration. Maybe she could still complete it before Beatrice's vision failed completely.

"*Alors,*" Beatrice said finally. "Later then, yes?"

Therese was in a daze when she hung up the phone, then hope set in, a new, exquisite form of torture. Would Beatrice tell Milo that she was going to finish the painting? Would Milo care? Would he call? Would he come with the picture?

The painting came with incredible speed, almost as if it had been flown over first class on the next plane. Therese stared at it a mere two days after the phone call with Beatrice, knowing even before she unwrapped the crate what she would find inside. Her assistant gazed at her with a puzzled expression as Therese bit her lip, staring.

"Is this that picture you were working on?" Kate asked. "Your horoscope said something big was happening today."

Therese nodded. "I don't think . . . I don't think I'll take a look at it right now. Why don't you just unwrap it to make sure it came over safely, then we'll store it until I can get to it."

Kate obligingly set to with a crowbar, and Therese sat back at her table, her nerves grating with every sound behind her so that she was entirely unable to concentrate on the triptych before her.

"Oh! Come see!" Kate called, and Therese was beside her in a flash.

There Louisa was, as radiant and peaceful as ever. Therese gazed at her lovely face as if at an old friend, and her hands lovingly touched the edges of the portrait. She looked at the pearl and shook her head. They'd been careful. A restorer had delicately removed as little of the paint as possible, but even so it had ruined the pearl. She held a hand over it, blocking the destruction from her view, and her eyes filled with tears as she looked again at the beautiful, pure face.

It's like having your heart cut out, isn't it? she thought. Everything else looks just the same, but the heart is gone.

"You okay?" Kate asked.

Therese turned away, sniffling and wiping once at her eyes. "I just need some air," she said.

She couldn't help it. She had been hoping Milo would bring the painting himself. Despite everything, she had believed he might be there.

She hurried down the hallway and burst through the outside door to the light and warmth of spring, to the sound of distant laughter. A bus full of schoolchildren was unloading at the curb and she walked rapidly away from them toward the park, seeking the solitude of the water and the trees, following the path she had taken once before with Milo.

Her heart was pounding, her throat dry and raw from the urge to cry, but she fought back the tears. She could feel the sunlight prickly and warm on her sweater, and her feet automatically turned into the rose garden, a peaceful, walled area where gravel paths guided her through rows of roses just showing their first buds. Even this place was bittersweet for her, because she remembered wanting to be there with Milo. It seemed so long ago since they had walked just outside this wall.

She had reached down to touch a tight dark bud, when she heard a sound behind her and looked up over her shoulder.

Disbelief shot through her. Milo Dansforth was walking slowly along the gravel path, his brow furrowed, his mouth unsmiling. Her lungs expanded with joy, then tightened with pain. She straightened and held herself as tall as she could, tilting her face to hold his gaze.

"I thought it was you," he said as he came nearer. "I was going into the museum, but then I saw you . . ."

His voice faltered and stopped.

He was thinner, she saw, almost gaunt around the cheeks and jaw. His dark hair was cut shorter, a little too short. The leather coat was gone and in its place was a thick white sweater, one of those Scottish ones that always made her want to touch the ropy pattern. And khaki trousers, she saw, her gaze dropping lower. She noted his worn leather shoes and tried to calculate how many steps it would take her to be in his arms. Two. If he wanted her.

His expression was so guarded, she couldn't tell what he was thinking, and she didn't know how he'd react to all the things she'd been thinking about. She didn't know how to start.

"Beatrice sent the painting back to me," she said.

"I know. She told me she'd talked to you."

Her fingers curled anxiously away from the rosebud, and she hid them in the pocket of her blue and gray print dress, hunching as a cool breeze wafted over the wall.

"Did you come to check on your house?" she asked.

"In a way."

The sunlight played on his shoulders and elbows, on the top of his head, where the newly cut hair lay with keen edges. Every inch of him appealed to her fingertips, but she kept them frozen in her pockets and waited for him to explain.

His gaze was steady, unwavering.

"How long is this silence going to go on?" he asked simply.

"Oh, Milo. It's been so awful. Why didn't you call me?"

"How could I?" he said. "I'm the most egotistical of men, remember?"

She winced. "I'm sorry."

"Really?"

"Of course. I never should have said that, no matter how true it was. And now I—"

She broke off as Milo erupted with laughter.

"Monster," he said.

She felt her lungs expand with hope again. "You were so insufferably right about so many things," she said. "It's taken me ages to put it all together, and it just makes me squirm to think I have to compromise my 'art before everything else' motto for life. What else do I have to go on now?"

He grinned again, sliding his hands into his pockets. "I don't know. Something more humble, I suppose."

"And I suppose you have a suggestion."

He shrugged. "I might."

She peered up at him, waiting. He, in turn, cleared his throat and frowned down at his shoes. A pair of robins flew overhead and beyond the wall, and Therese heard chirping from a nearby nest.

"What do you think of Louisa?" he asked.

The question caught her off guard.

"Louisa looks awful," she said, "like her heart was ripped out."

He nodded slowly. "It was worth it, though. The search under the pearl transformed Beatrice. I don't know why, but she had focused all the loneliness of her life into finding her grandmother's bequest. Now she's a different person. More at peace, and more generous. She doesn't even want the ring back from Thomas."

"I know. She told me."

He studied her for a moment.

"Isn't her peace worth the price of a painted pearl?" he asked.

She pulled her black braid forward and gazed down at the ground. "Yes," she said quietly. "That's worth it."

She could sense Milo relaxing.

"So we really did do the right thing. And you can fix it up again," he said. "So no one can ever tell except yourself."

"Just as you predicted."

"Yes."

Now if she could only fix up her own heart so easily, she thought.

Another breeze eased up the path, lifting a strand of black hair free from behind her ear so that it crossed her eyes. She smoothed it back, acutely aware of the way he was watching her, his gaze lingering on her cheek, her hair, until she could almost feel his touch there. She had missed being with him, but in a way this was worse. Was he really content to simply reach a resolution about their last fight, when she wanted so much more?

The strain of the silence was more than she could bear.

"Is that all you came to tell me?" she asked.

"There was one other thing," he said.

She watched his eyes grow dark with emotion, and his eyebrows drew together.

"Therese, it was never a charade."

Her heart knocked savagely in her chest, and she had to lock her suddenly unreliable knees.

"What do you mean?" she asked.

He angled his face slightly. "You've had time to think about us. If you don't know now, you never will."

She caught her breath and felt a rush of emotion. She looked at the love in his expression, the hope and fear that shone from his eyes, and in one short step she reached for him.

For one instant longer he held back, so they could both be certain she'd reached for him first, then he crushed her in his arms.

"My God, Therese," he murmured against her hair. "What a ride you've put me through."

"I was coming to Paris tomorrow," she said. "I've got a ticket and everything."

He straightened and she looked up into his face, smiling at his surprised expression.

"You were really going to come and find me?" he asked.

"I decided even before I heard from Beatrice. But I didn't know if you'd still want me."

He pulled her so close her toes lifted off the gravel,

and he kissed her so hard she lost her breath and had to break off with a laugh. She loved the faint smile creases around his mouth, the lean lines of his cheeks and jaw.

"I want to hear about this," he said. "I thought you'd still be furious with me. Or indifferent."

"Ha!" She laughed. "Indifferent. That's good."

She tried to tell him her thoughts about her father and her slow realization that she'd let art and her own work blind her to larger issues of trust and love. "I didn't know I was doing it," she said.

"I knew how you felt about your work," he said. "That's why I wanted you to do the restoration in the first place. I knew you valued art more than anything and that you'd never do anything as uncouth as dig for the emeralds with a garden trowel."

She cringed again. "You have a most inconvenient memory," she said.

He laughed. "I like the way your cheeks get pink when you're filled with remorse."

That got her. "Listen. I was not the only person at fault here. You were the one who threw the matter of getting a second opinion in my face. Talk about insulting." She mimicked a tough voice. "Stuff this down your throat, miss."

"I've been known to have more tact," he admitted.

Her laughter went merrily down the rose garden.

"You're going to marry me," he said. "Right away."

She grabbed both his hands and laughed again. She loved having him so close, knowing at any second she could pull him near or that he would pull her in. It was a game of light and happiness just waiting to see how long they could remain apart. And their whole lives would be that way, she could feel it.

"Ah, excuse me," he said. "Did I hear a yes?"

She raised her eyebrows slightly. "I didn't realize that you had proposed. I thought you were just practicing that masterful tone of yours."

He slid gracefully down onto one knee and presented an innocent, earnest face, completely unlike his usual roguish expression. He was so tall that even kneeling, his face was only slightly lower than her own. Then she felt his strong fingers tighten their grip on her hands, and he simply gazed up at her with an intimacy that deepened with each passing second.

Was this someone she could spend her life with?

Better to ask if she could bear to live without him.

"You didn't need to worry if I'd still want you," he said. "I'll always want you, with every ounce of wanting that I have. You're like the secrets in my own heart, already a part of me." He pressed her hands against his chest. "Will you marry me, Therese? Will you love me, and have children with me, and grow old with me?"

He was offering her a reality beyond her most precious dreams, and she didn't think she could ever be happier. "Can we start now?" she asked.

She tugged at his hands, then slid into his embrace as he stood. Her body instinctively molded against his, and deep within her she felt an expansive warmth of contentment and security. Then, as his lips touched hers, the light coiling of desire began to twist inside her and she knew she wanted to be intimate with him soon. She couldn't wait to see what it would be like to make love with him now that she fully understood her feelings for him, now that she could show him inch by inch how much she loved him.

Through the thin fabric of her dress, her breasts were pressed against the patterned wool of his sweater, and she could feel his hands spanning her waist, holding her tight against him. She pivoted slightly, rubbing her body against his, and heard a rumble deep in his throat. His kiss deepened, and she melted, leaving all issues of balance and gravity up to him.

"I've missed you," he said.

He loosened his arms just enough to cradle her against him, and she smiled, his embrace providing a circle of warmth against the cool breeze. The sunlight was brilliant on the rosebuds around them, and Therese breathed deep, smelling the rich earth and sweet aroma of new life. The glorious day seemed to mirror the happiness she felt with Milo, making her feel infectiously alive.

Suddenly he laughed. "Here I am surrounded by roses, without one to give you."

She gazed up lovingly, a slow, sweet smile easing onto her lips. "Think you can ever make it up to me?"

He touched his mouth to hers, then moved to her ear, where she felt the soft caress of his voice. "Something like that," he said.

THE EDITORS' CORNER

Shake off those stuffy winter doldrums and get ready for the first scents of spring, which are sure to charm you into going outside. But don't forget to pack the new April LOVESWEPTs in your picnic basket. We have some of your favorite authors delivering terrifically unique, terrifically LOVESWEPT stories that are guaranteed to make springtime bloom in your heart. Enjoy!

Logan Blackstone plays **DARK KNIGHT** to Scottie Giardi's secret agent in Donna Kauffman's steamy new LOVESWEPT, #882. Scottie has a mission to accomplish—to keep Logan busy so that he can't interfere with a covert plan that's been in motion for months. But Logan has plans of his own. He's on the hunt for his long-lost twin brother, Lucas, who's involved in a cult. Stuck together in a cabin, the two form a tenuous relationship of passion and respect, not to mention constant bickering and bantering. Logan and Scottie are two kindred souls who are running from themselves, but will they acknowledge that it's time to stop fearing yesterday and look forward to tomorrow? Donna Kauffman answers that question in this achingly intense story of perfectly matched adversaries.

In Kathy Lynn Emerson's new LOVESWEPT, #883, Chase Forster and Leslie Baynton promise to be together **SIGHT UNSEEN.** Convinced by her sister that she's become the stereotypical old-maid librarian, complete with feline companion, Leslie knows it's time for a change in her life. So when Chase sends an E-mail asking, "Will you be my E-mail-order bride?" Leslie answers with a very uncharacteristic yes. Granted, getting married to a man she's met only by computer is a little crazy, but as soon as she hears Chase's warm voice, she knows she's made the right decision. Chase has to raise his brother's children and he thinks Leslie would make a terrific role model for the troubled teens. So a makeshift family is born. With more than a few surprises up her sleeve, Kathy explores the intricacies of a thoroughly modern marriage.

Well-received author Kristen Robinette brings us **FLIRTING WITH FIRE,** LOVESWEPT #884. Danger had Samantha Delaney on the run, and after coming to live in the small southern town of Scottsdale, Georgia, she thought for sure that she had escaped its clutches. Samantha answers Daniel Caldwell's ad for an apartment for rent and moves into the east wing of his antebellum home. Daniel, with a secret of his own locked away in the caretaker's cottage, wonders at the demons haunting his lovely tenant's eyes. Suddenly the threats are back and Samantha no longer knows who she can turn to—her devastatingly handsome landlord or her faithful and loyal assistant. Kristen Robinette weaves an intricate and suspenseful tale that is as emotionally compelling as it is exquisitely romantic.

In Jill Shalvis's **THE HARDER THEY FALL**, LOVESWEPT #885, Trisha Mallory falls out of the ceiling into Dr. Hunter Adams's arms, and thus begins a stormy relationship that makes for great laughs and huge catastrophes. Whether she's forgetting to close refrigerator doors or rearranging his car's fender, Trisha seems to wreak havoc wherever she goes. And for Hunter, a stuffy space scientist (Trisha's words, not ours), having Trisha as a neighbor is going to be the end of him. After living with incredibly flighty parents, Hunter has vowed that never again will his life be unorganized, while Trisha has vowed that the effects of her strict upbringing will not cloud her zest for life. Jill Shalvis's fast-paced romp pairs two mismatched lovers who are stunned to discover they're mad for each other.

Happy reading!

With warmest wishes,

Susann Brailey

Joy Abella

Susann Brailey
Senior Editor

Joy Abella
Administrative Editor

P.S. Look for these women's fiction titles coming in April! Dubbed by *USA Today* as "one of the hottest and most prolific romance writers today," *New York Times* bestseller Amanda Quick delivers **WITH THIS RING,** in which a villain lurks in the netherworld of London, waiting for authoress Beatrice Poole and the Earl of Monkcrest to unearth the Forbidden Rings—knowing that when they do, that day will be their last. Now available in paperback is *New York Times* bestseller Tami Hoag's **A THIN DARK LINE,** a breathtakingly sensual novel filled with heart-stopping suspense when the boundaries between the law and justice and love and murder are crossed. From nationally bestselling Teresa Medeiros comes a new romance blockbuster, **NOBODY'S DARLING.** When young Bostonian Esmerelda Fine hires her brother's accused murderer to help track her brother down, the adventure and passion have just begun. . . . Bantam newcomer Katie Rose presents **A HINT OF MISCHIEF.** Three beautiful sisters set Victorian New York society—and a sinfully attractive businessman—on its ear when they start performing séances, in this clever historical romance of nineteenth-century America. And immediately following this page, preview the Bantam women's fiction titles on sale in March!

For current information on Bantam's women's fiction, visit our Web site, *Isn't It Romantic,* at the following address: **http://www.bdd.com/romance**

Don't miss these extraordinary
novels from Bantam Books!

On Sale in March:

PUBLIC SECRETS
by Nora Roberts

BIRTHDAY GIRLS
by Jean Stone

SHOTGUN GROOM
by Sandra Chastain

"Move over, Sidney Sheldon: the world has a new
master of romantic suspense, and her name is
Nora Roberts."—Rex Reed

Emma, beautiful, intelligent, radiantly talented,
she lives in a star-studded world of wealth and
privilege. But she is about to discover that fame is
no protection at all when someone wants
you dead. . . .

PUBLIC SECRETS
by Nora Roberts

*All she has to do is close her eyes and remember the day
Brian McAvoy swept into her life. A frightened toddler, she didn't know then that she was his illegitimate
daughter or that he was pop music's rising star. All she
knew was that with Brian, his band mates, and his
new wife, she felt safe. And when her baby brother
arrived, Emma thought she was the luckiest girl in the
world . . . until the night a botched kidnapping attempt shattered all their lives . . . and destroyed
Emma's happiness.*

*Yet now, even though Emma is still haunted by
flashes of memory from that fateful night, she has survived. She's carved out a thrilling career and even
dared to fall rapturously in love. But the man who will
become her husband isn't all that he seems. And
Emma is about to awaken to the chilling knowledge
that the darkest secret of all is the one buried in her
mind—a secret that someone may kill to keep.*

When Emma woke, the floor was vibrating with the bass from the stereo. She lay quietly a moment listening, trying as she did from time to time to recognize the song from the beat alone.

She'd gotten used to the parties. Her da liked to have people around. Lots of music, lots of laughing. When she was older, she would go to parties, too.

Bev always made sure the house was very clean before the guests arrived. That was silly, really, Emma thought. In the morning, the house was a terrible mess with smelly glasses and overflowing ashtrays. More often than not a few of the guests would be sprawled over the sofas and chairs amid the clutter.

Emma wondered what it would be like to sit up all night, talking, laughing, listening to music. When you were grown up, no one told you when you had to go to bed, or have a bath.

With a sigh, she rolled over on her back. The music was faster now. She could feel the driving bass pulse in the walls. And something else. Footsteps, coming down the hall, Emma thought. Miss Wallingsford. She prepared to close her eyes and feign sleep when another thought occurred to her. Perhaps it was Da or Mum passing through to check on her and Darren. If it was, she could pretend to have just woken, then she could persuade them to tell her about the party.

But the footsteps passed by. She sat up clutching Charlie. She'd wanted company, even if only for a moment or two. She wanted to talk about the party, or the trip to New York. She wanted to know what song was playing. She sat a moment, a small, sleepy child in a pink nightgown, bathed by the cheerful glow of a Mickey Mouse night-light.

She thought she heard Darren crying. Straightening, she strained to listen. She was certain she heard Darren's cranky tears over the pulse of the music. Automatically she climbed out of bed, tucking Charlie under one arm. She would sit with Darren until he quieted, and leave Charlie to watch over him through the rest of the night.

The hallway was dark, which surprised her. A light always burned there in case Emma had to use the bathroom during the night. She had a bad moment at the doorway, imagining the things that lurked in the shadowy corners. She wanted to stay in her room with the grinning Mickey.

Then Darren let out a yowling cry.

There was nothing in the corners, Emma told herself as she started down the dark hallway. There was nothing there at all. No monsters, no ghosts, no squishy or slithering things.

It was the Beatles playing now.

Emma wet her lips. Just the dark, just the dark, she told herself. Her eyes had adjusted to the dark by the time she'd reached Darren's door. It was closed. That was wrong, too. His door was always left open so he could be heard easily when awakened.

She reached out, then jumped as she thought she heard something move behind her. Heart pumping, she turned to scan the dark hallway. Shifting shadows towered into nameless monsters, making sweat break out on her brow and back.

Nothing there, nothing there, she told herself, and Darren was crying his lungs out.

She turned the knob and pushed the door open.

"Come together," Lennon sang. "Over me."

There were two men in the room. One was holding Darren, struggling to keep him still while the baby screamed in fear and anger. The other had something in his hand, something that the light from the giraffe lamp on the dresser caused to glint.

"What are you doing?"

The man whirled at her voice. He wasn't a doctor, Emma thought as she made out the needle in his hand. She recognized him, and knew he wasn't a doctor. And Darren wasn't sick.

The other man swore, a short spurt of ugly words, while he fought to keep Darren from wriggling out of his arms.

"Emma," the man she knew said in a calm, friendly voice. He smiled. It was a false smile, an angry smile. She noted it, and that he still held the needle as he stepped toward her. She turned and ran.

Behind her she heard Darren call out. "*Ma!*"

Sobbing, she raced down the hall. There were monsters, her panicked mind taunted. There were monsters and things with snappy teeth in the shadows. They were coming after her now.

He nearly caught the trailing edge of her nightgown. Swearing, he dove for her. His hand skimmed over her ankle, slid off. She yelped as though she'd been scalded. As she reached the top of the stairs, she screamed for her father, shrieking his name over and over again.

Then her legs tangled. She tumbled down the flight of stairs.

In the kitchen, someone sat on the counter and ordered fifty pizzas. Shaking her head, Bev checked the freezer for ice. No one used more ice than Americans. As an afterthought, she dropped a cube in her warming wine. When in Rome, she decided, then turned toward the door.

She met Brian on the threshold.

Grinning, he hooked an arm around her waist and gave her a long, lazy kiss. "Hi."

"Hi." Still holding the wine, she linked her hands behind his neck. "Bri."

"Hmm?"

"Who are all these people?"

He laughed, nuzzling into her neck. "You've got me." The scent of her had him hardening. Moving to the sinuous beat of the Lennon/McCartney number, he brought her against him. "What do you say we take a trip upstairs and leave them the rest of the house."

"That's rude." But she moved against him. "Wicked, rude, and the best idea I've heard in hours."

"Well, then . . ." He made a halfhearted attempt to pick her up, sent them both teetering. Wine spilled cool down his back as Bev giggled. "Maybe you can carry me," he said, then heard Emma scream.

He rammed into a small table as he turned. Dizzy from drugs and booze, he stumbled, righted himself, and rushed into the foyer. There were people already gathered. Pushing through them, he saw her crumpled at the foot of the steps.

"Emma. My God." He was terrified to touch her. There was blood at the corner of her mouth. With one trembling finger, he wiped it away. He looked up into a sea of faces, a blur of color, all unrecognizable. His stomach clenched, then tried to heave itself into his throat.

"Call an ambulance," he managed, then bent over her again.

"Don't move her." Bev's face was chalk-white as she knelt beside him. "I don't think you're supposed to move her. We need a blanket." Some quick-witted soul was already thrusting a daisy afghan into her hands. "She'll be all right, Bri." Carefully, Bev smoothed the blanket over her. "She'll be just fine."

He closed his eyes, shook his head to clear it. But when he opened them again, Emma was still lying, dead-white, on the floor. There was too much noise. The music echoing off the ceilings, the voices murmuring, muttering all around. He felt a hand on his shoulder. A quick, reassuring squeeze.

"Ambulance is on the way," P.M. told him. "Hold on, Bri."

"Get them out," he whispered. He looked up and into Johnno's shocked, pale face. "Get them out of here."

With a nod, Johnno began to urge people along. The door was open, the night bright with floodlights and headlights when they heard the wail of the sirens.

"I'm going to go up," Bev said calmly. "Tell Alice what's happened, check on Darren. We'll go to the hospital with her. She's going to be fine, Brian. I know it."

He could only nod and stare down at Emma's still, pale face. He couldn't leave her. If he had dared, he would have gone into the bathroom, stuck a finger down his throat, and tried to rid his body of some of the chemicals he'd pumped into it that night.

It was all like a dream, he thought, a floaty, unhappy dream. Until he looked at Emma's face. Then it was real, much too real.

The *Abbey Road* album was still playing, the sly cut about murder. Maxwell's silver hammer was coming down.

"Bri." Johnno put a hand on his arm. "Move back now, so they can tend to her."

"What?"

"Move back." Gently Johnno eased him to his feet. "They need to have a look at her."

Dazed, Brian watched the ambulance attendants move in and crouch over his daughter. "She must have fallen all the way down the stairs."

"She'll be all right." Johnno sent a helpless look toward P.M. as they flanked Brian. "Little girls are tougher than they look."

"That's right." A bit unsteady on his feet, Stevie stood behind Brian with both hands on his shoulders. "Our Emma won't let a tumble down the stairs hold her up for long."

"We'll go to the hospital with you." Pete moved over to join them. Together they watched as Emma was carefully lifted onto a stretcher.

Upstairs, Bev screamed . . . and screamed and screamed, until the sound filled every corner of the house.

A gifted storyteller who truly "understands the human heart,"* Jean Stone returns with another deeply enthralling tale, this one about three women facing fifty—and determined to change their lives. . . .

BIRTHDAY GIRLS
by Jean Stone

Once they were childhood friends who celebrated birthdays together, sharing laughter and tears and heartfelt dreams. Then they lost touch. Yet now, on the brink of turning fifty, one of them is desperate enough to contact the others—looking for more than an innocent reunion. . . .

Abigail is a star, a new Martha Stewart whose weekly TV show has won her millions of fans. Maddie is a brilliant photographer under contract with a hip magazine. And daredevil Kris is a writer whose taut thrillers have been on bestseller lists for years. But one of them carries a dark, tormenting secret; another is obsessed with the man she loved and lost; a third would give anything to start over; and all are haunted by the stark passage of time.

So what will the friends do? They'll share their birthday wishes just like before, only this time they'll go to any lengths to make sure their wishes come true. . . .

* The Literary Times

"It would be nice if one of you said something."

Maddie realized she was staring at Abigail— the woman who had everything any woman in the world could possibly ever want, except, of course, kids; but then again, Kris hadn't wanted any either but now she did and, oh God, this was all so confusing it made her head hurt. She blinked. "Maybe you should clarify."

Kris laughed. "I think our queen of the kitchen is saying she wants out."

"*Out*," Abigail said. "Yes, that's a good word. All my life I've been trying to please others. First it was Grandfather. Then Edmund. Now the entire freaking world."

Maddie watched as Abigail walked over to the fireplace, ran her finger across the carved marble mantel, then looked up to the portraits of her grandfather and his father before him. It struck her that this was not the same, unretouched woman who posed on the cover of *In the Rose Garden with Abigail*; this was not the same woman who had always been in control. She was pale and drawn; she was . . . vulnerable. God, in all the years Maddie had known her, she'd never once thought of Abigail Hardy as vulnerable.

"I don't even have a clue who I am," Abigail said softly. "By the time I am fifty I need to find out. But I'm not going to learn it by pretending to be someone I no longer want to be."

Maddie now realized that Abigail must definitely have hit menopause. It was the only answer that made any sense. She tried to sound compassionate as she asked, "Have you seen a gynecologist?"

Abigail whipped around. "Don't blame my hormones, Maddie. I've hated every minute of my life for years. Most of all, I hate the damn 'empire' I worked so hard to create. Now I'm going to do something about it."

It was difficult to believe that Abigail was serious. She had done so much with her life, had touched so many people. How would millions of women react without Abigail Hardy in their kitchens each week? How would Sophie react? Maddie wanted to ask if there would be reruns, but somehow that didn't seem appropriate. Still, the thought of no longer having to endure the dinner-of-the-week was not unappealing.

Kris stood and moved over to Abigail. "I say go for it, girl. What the hell, we only live once."

"Thanks, Kris. I knew I could count on you."

Maddie wondered what Betty Ann would have said, in her cherub-like, childlike way. "Maybe you should take it a step at a time," she replied, trying to sound encouraging. "Start with a separation from Edmund. Cut down on your work schedule. Travel. Something less . . . drastic." Her words sounded thin. She traced the curves of the paisley brocade on the sofa.

"I don't think you get it, Maddie. This isn't like a diet. I'm not trying to wean myself off chocolate. If I'm going to do this, I've got to do it. Sever the ties. All of them."

"Including divorce?" Maddie asked.

"Sorry, Maddie," Kris said. "Sometimes that's what it takes to move on."

But Abigail was shaking her head. "No. I'm not going to get a divorce."

"What then?" Maddie asked.

"I'm going to disappear. And you are going to help me fake my death."

Kris whistled. "Holy shit, you're serious."

Abigail raised her chin. "Very."

"You can't do that," Maddie protested. "You can't just drop off the face of the earth and make people think you're . . . dead."

"It's the only way. My life is too complicated. Untangling the business alone would be a nightmare. And it could take years."

It hadn't taken years for Parker to "untangle" Maddie from *Our World*. A few swipes of the pen on the dotted line and—presto—she was out. Of course, the magazine had still been in its infancy. Of course, there had been no profits to make it look valuable. Of course, Maddie had been stupid.

"You two are the only ones I can trust," Abigail continued. "No one but the three of us can know the truth. Maddie gets her ex-husband, Kris gets her baby, and I get . . . out. It's all or nothing. Do we have a deal?"

Maddie chanced a glance at Kris. Kris grinned back at her. So Abigail *had* had an agenda. Now they knew. "When do you plan to do this?"

"Not until your wishes have come true. Unless, of course, either of you changes her mind. I, for one, won't."

The irony did not escape Maddie. Here she was, trying to get her life back, and here Abigail was, trying to throw hers away. As for Kris, well, who knew about Kris. Next week she'd probably be off in Bora Bora and forget the whole thing.

"So," Kris asked, "where do we start?"

"Maddie made her wish first, so let's begin with her."

"That should be easy," Kris said. "Men are my specialty."

Folding her hands in her lap, Maddie wondered which one of them was the craziest.

From
Sandra Chastain,
bestselling author of
Raven and the Cowboy, comes

SHOTGUN GROOM

A Tennessee belle with her sights aimed at a rugged Texan's heart, Lily Towns was determined to marry Matt Logan, even if she had to use her shotgun to get him to the altar. But confirmed bachelor Matt Logan wasn't looking for a bride, especially one sexy, sensual Memphis belle.

When the only woman on the coach stepped down onto the plank sidewalk at the stage office, Matt knew immediately that it was too late to whisk her away. This was one time his private business was likely to become public. Drawing Racer to a stop behind a stack of wooden kegs, he sat helplessly watching the woman smile at everyone in sight.

"Welcome to Blue Station," Luther said, his head bobbing like a chicken picking up corn.

"Yes, ma'am," Ambrose Wells, the town's self-appointed mayor, said, suddenly appearing on the platform as if meeting the stage were part of the banker's everyday duties. "I'm the president of the Blue Station Banking Company, Miss . . ."

"Townsend, Miss Lillian Townsend. I'm so very pleased to meet . . . all of you."

Lillian Townsend? Even the name was much

too elegant for the Double L. Lillian Townsend ought to be one of those entertainers who traveled around making stage appearances, instead of this elegant vision of sunlight and satin who'd come here to be a Texas bride.

"And what brings you to Blue Station, Miss Townsend?" Wells asked, still holding her hand as if he didn't trust the good fortune that brought such a beauty to town. "Is someone meeting you?"

"Oh yes, I'm being met by my future husband."

The expression on the banker's face froze and he looked at Luther in disbelief. Matt swore silently from his vantage point.

Apparently Luther hadn't shared the information that Matt Logan was getting married, though he had obviously told Wells a new woman was coming on the stage. But Lillian Townsend was about to spread the news.

"Future husband?" Wells questioned, not bothering to conceal his surprise.

"Why, yes. Matt Logan. He and his brother, Jim, have a cattle ranch nearby, I believe."

Christ! Now she'd done it. Matt had always been a very private man, keeping himself away from involvement with the townspeople. He'd claimed that there were no women in Blue Springs, but that hadn't been entirely true. There were women, too many women, and their constant matchmaking made his life miserable.

Now this woman was announcing to the world that she'd come to marry one of the Logan brothers. Matt had to stop her quick.

On Sale in April:

WITH THIS RING
by *Amanda Quick*

A THIN
DARK LINE
by *Tami Hoag*

NOBODY'S
DARLING
by *Teresa Medeiros*

A HINT
OF MISCHIEF
by *Katie Rose*

Bestselling Historical Women's Fiction

⚜ AMANDA QUICK ⚜

____28354-5 SEDUCTION ...$6.50/$8.99 Canada

____28932-2 SCANDAL ....$6.50/$8.99

____28594-7 SURRENDER ....$6.50/$8.99

____29325-7 RENDEZVOUS ....$6.50/$8.99

____29315-X RECKLESS ....$6.50/$8.99

____29316-8 RAVISHED ....$6.50/$8.99

____29317-6 DANGEROUS ....$6.50/$8.99

____56506-0 DECEPTION ....$6.50/$8.99

____56153-7 DESIRE ....$6.50/$8.99

____56940-6 MISTRESS ....$6.50/$8.99

____57159-1 MYSTIQUE ....$6.50/$7.99

____57190-7 MISCHIEF ....$6.50/$8.99

____57407-8 AFFAIR ....$6.99/$8.99

⚜ IRIS JOHANSEN ⚜

____29871-2 LAST BRIDGE HOME ...$5.50/$7.50

____29604-3 THE GOLDEN

BARBARIAN ....$6.99/$8.99

____29244-7 REAP THE WIND ......$5.99/$7.50

____29032-0 STORM WINDS ....$6.99/$8.99

- -

Ask for these books at your local bookstore or use this page to order.

Please send me the books I have checked above. I am enclosing $____ (add $2.50 to cover postage and handling). Send check or money order, no cash or C.O.D.'s, please.

Name _____

Address _____

City/State/Zip _____

Send order to: Bantam Books, Dept. FN 16, 2451 S. Wolf Rd., Des Plaines, IL 60018
Allow four to six weeks for delivery.

Prices and availability subject to change without notice.   FN 16 3/98

Bestselling Historical Women's Fiction

⚜ IRIS JOHANSEN ⚜

____28855-5 THE WIND DANCER . . .$5.99/$6.99

____29968-9 THE TIGER PRINCE . . .$6.99/$8.99

____29944-1 THE MAGNIFICENT

                ROGUE . . . .$6.99/$8.99

____29945-X BELOVED SCOUNDREL .$6.99/$8.99

____29946-8 MIDNIGHT WARRIOR . .$6.99/$8.99

____29947-6 DARK RIDER . . . .$6.99/$8.99

____56990-2 LION'S BRIDE . . . .$6.99/$8.99

____56991-0 THE UGLY DUCKLING. . .$5.99/$7.99

____57181-8 LONG AFTER MIDNIGHT.$6.99/$8.99

____10616-3 AND THEN YOU DIE.... $22.95/$29.95

⚜ TERESA MEDEIROS ⚜

____29407-5 HEATHER AND VELVET .$5.99/$7.50

____29409-1 ONCE AN ANGEL . . . . . .$5.99/$7.99

____29408-3 A WHISPER OF ROSES .$5.99/$7.99

____56332-7 THIEF OF HEARTS . . . . .$5.50/$6.99

____56333-5 FAIREST OF THEM ALL .$5.99/$7.50

____56334-3 BREATH OF MAGIC . . . .$5.99/$7.99

____57623-2 SHADOWS AND LACE . . .$5.99/$7.99

____57500-7 TOUCH OF

            ENCHANTMENT. . . . .$5.99/$7.99

- -

Ask for these books at your local bookstore or use this page to order.

Please send me the books I have checked above. I am enclosing $____ (add $2.50 to cover postage and handling). Send check or money order, no cash or C.O.D.'s, please.

Name _____

Address _____

City/State/Zip _____

Send order to: Bantam Books, Dept. FN 16, 2451 S. Wolf Rd., Des Plaines, IL 60018
Allow four to six weeks for delivery.
Prices and availability subject to change without notice.   FN 16 3/98